CW00371566

THE
JUSTICE
QUOTIENT

THE
JUSTICE
QUOTIENT

THE FINAL OUTPOST

PHILIP ALTMAN

To order additional copies of this book, contact:
Xlibris
800-056-3182
www.Xlibrispublishing.co.uk
Orders@Xlibrispublishing.co.uk
784716

In memory of my very dear family and friends.

This book concludes the trilogy which began with 2056: Meltdown (9781543488432) and continued with The Alien Veil (9781543490725).

CHAPTER ONE

So it wasn't surprising that they wondered what had gone wrong. One moment, everything seemed to be under control; and the next minute, pandemonium had broken out in the building where Viktor and his son Ben had previously carried on their spying business and which had then been turned into a visitors' museum after they had been closed down.

The place was suddenly filled with alien beings who were supposed to have all been evicted from Earth! Obviously, the portal in the international space veil, meant to be secure and under proper control, had been breached. It was a disastrous situation all round, and there was panic everywhere when they saw what had happened.

Then the humans started to wonder if it was just possible. They knew, as everyone had got to hear, that what was left of the power in the museum's systems had been sufficient to resurrect the body of the dead judgebot, which had been kept in the court cupboard as a souvenir before weirdly taking itself up to the bench to hear the next case. So the question now was, What else might those residual power impulses have caused elsewhere in the world, let alone just in London?

These were just a few of the questions faced by the prime minister, who led his investigative PMG group. He knew his own limitations, and these were quite obviously very technical problems with which he needed help solving.

He'd come from a poor background himself, where matters of that sort never cropped up, although space matters had always intrigued him even from when he was a small boy. He would get hold of every magazine he could find dealing with extraterrestrials and space travel. Nevertheless, this was an entirely different situation, and he now felt the need to call together another meeting of his specialist Prime Minister's Group (known as the PMG) to seek some fresh expert ideas from its members.

It was 2086, and this was going to be completely fresh ground—having to cope with actual extraterrestrials and not the fictional ones from novels—so they needed all the help they could get, he realised.

He was convinced there was far too much at stake to get it wrong, bearing in mind the seemingly strong possibility that extraterrestrials might well have got in and be already roaming Earth, causing havoc everywhere that they had established themselves because of their unusual ways, practices, and appearance.

He opened the meeting of his PMG group by recounting the strange and eerie event that had taken place in the courtroom, when the body of the judgebot had suddenly come to life in the cupboard and had shakily taken itself over to sit on the judge's bench, seemingly ready to hear another case, and the extraordinary goings-on they found when they had gone back to the museum to check things out.

He continued with practical matters by asking if anyone had any idea if alien beings needed to eat and, if so, if anyone knew what sort of food they liked that might be available on Earth.

Everyone looked nonplussed. One delegate said that he had read that they do eat but only very small amounts, being very thin. But this had never been corroborated to his knowledge.

The prime minister said they should all go back to the museum to find out what was actually going on there and see if there was any sign of food about the place. That would be the first step, he told them.

Another delegate drew the obvious conclusion that if it was possible somehow to deprive them of food, then they would all die out anyway, but another wondered if their survival really did depend on food or maybe it wasn't actually essential for their kind. They agreed that they would have to find out, and very quickly too.

They were all soon at the museum only to find that it was completely locked up, with no one about. They thought this very strange. It was the middle of a weekday afternoon, and the official in charge should have been on duty but couldn't be found anywhere.

One of the delegates went round the corner of the building to have a look for another door on the off chance it might be unlocked and was astonished to find a man there moaning and in a great deal of distress, lying on the pavement, tied up!

When asked what had happened to him, he said that he was the official in charge of the museum and that three adult aliens had grabbed hold of him about two hours ago and had dragged him there, out of sight, next to the bins, without uttering a word to him!

He had then heard quite a lot of noise from the others as they had left the building and had come round the corner. For no reason at all, he said, rubbing his leg, they had kicked him as they went down the street, and he believed that they had all now left the museum, but he naturally had no idea where they'd gone to.

The prime minister came round the corner when called and saw to it that the museum keeper was released and cared for. He then asked him to open the place up so they could inspect it, especially looking for signs of food.

They all went round and were surprised that the aliens had locked the door when they'd left and, what is more, they'd taken the key with them! They had to summon up a locksmith, who got them in, and when they entered, they were astonished at what they found.

The whole place was in a shambles, display cabinets overturned and the museum's exhibits strewn across the floor, but what they were really looking for was any sign of food. And then they saw it. There were tiny bits of cheese about the place!

They asked the official how this could be. Did the place have mice? He replied that the museum had a cafe for visitors, that the selection of cheeses were kept in the fridge, and that he'd just had a fresh delivery only last week.

So they looked inside the fridge, and it became plain that the aliens had left everything else there untouched except the stock of cheese, which had virtually disappeared!

The official was very surprised that they'd eaten nearly all of it because there had been a very large amount in the fridge when he'd last looked. He explained that their cheese sandwiches were very popular with museum visitors, which is why they kept so much in stock.

So this was the way forward, the prime minister thought. They could either deprive the aliens of cheese or, better still, let them have it but poison it first! All they had to do was to find them in the first place!

·········●●●●●●●●●·········

They couldn't sensibly make a public announcement that extraterrestrial beings were somewhere out amongst the population but that they didn't know where they were now, could they? This was the dilemma the prime minister faced. So he asked his group for some suggestions how to go about dealing with these latest problems. How many were there, where had they got to, and how were they managing to get hold of food?

It could be, one of them suggested, that alien beings eat more than just cheese where they came from but that Earth didn't have the sort of this other food they were used to. Indeed, he said, it could be very useful for Man to know what else they did eat if he ever had to leave Earth for some reason in order to go to live out there, following some dire catastrophe befalling them.

CHAPTER TWO

· · · · ●●●●● ● ●●●●● · · · ·

Reports started coming in at London's central BT Tower that aliens had been spotted in different parts of the country. It was obvious to the PMG group, whose members were the best experts he could find, that they really needed to know how many they were going to have to deal with. Were they, for example, just in Britain or also in other countries around the world as well? No one knew.

It so happened that the major powers had held a meeting in Geneva just a few weeks before to consider what joint action they could take in the event of an invasion by extraterrestrials, and yet, just a short time later, they'd arrived!

A coordinated system of notification of any such incursions had been devised at that meeting, just in case. Coded messages were sent around the world from the Tower that some alien beings had broken through from space into the London area and that if any aliens had been discovered elsewhere, the information should be sent straight to London's BT Tower for analysis, where it could be properly coordinated. But on no account should the population be allowed to become frightened so far as it was possible, that is, because they should be told that the problem could soon be brought under control.

Dealing with this major event was clearly going to require a speedy and coordinated worldwide effort to eradicate them before they settled down and reproduced themselves beyond measure. The whole exercise would require unprecedented international cooperation if they were to stand any chance of succeeding and not being pushed out from living on Earth.

The prime minister set up a special sub-department deep down in the Tower solely to deal with this potentially enormous threat to our world, and he assigned his best people to run it.

The first thing they did was to send out more coded messages, this time about what they had discovered at the museum about the cheese that had obviously been used for their food and asking them to send back any specific reports about any unusual occurrences they'd encountered.

Some recipients were quite amused at first hearing about the cheese, just as those who'd discovered it had been, but it soon dawned on them that this information could well be the way to eradicating the aliens from Earth.

So far as the insecure portal in the international veil protecting Earth was concerned, it was clear that this was indeed a major problem. Some said that it should be closed down permanently. Others said that this idea wasn't sensible because the portal had its essential uses; its security just needed to be severely tightened up, monitored properly, and then kept that way.

Then one of the PMG group's older delegates remembered how friendly and helpful the alien being named Yost had been when specialised space knowledge was required.

The prime minister was pleasantly reminded by him of the episode when Yost had helped Zooba to create the international space veil in the first place to keep out the alien beings and the time when he had frightened the extraterrestrials not to settle on Earth because he had told them of disease and microbes here, none of which they liked the sound of, and had soon fled.

He addressed the PMG group at its next meeting in their secure room in Parliament and said, 'I think we should ask Zooba to get in touch with Yost on the transponder he's given him and to tell him only a suitable part of what has taken place. Telling him of the breach of the portal, he would draw the conclusion that all of Yost's warnings of disease and the like had obviously not reached those who'd got through and were still on Earth, and we should ask him if he could suggest how to help Zooba with this new incursion.'

Yost had always been concerned to help Zooba ever since he'd been kind to him and hopefully would be happy to do so again, so the meeting agreed, and it then broke up, generally feeling that good progress had been made.

CHAPTER THREE

········●●●●●●●●●●·····

Sitting alone in the country mansion in southern England which the Government had given him for services rendered to his country, Zooba was bored out of his mind. He always tried to be on the go mentally, but so far as any actual activity was concerned, it was non-existent because he'd developed a bad leg after tripping on a stone when out walking in a nearby field.

Though country living was always made out to be very desirable by the locals whom he'd got to know, he just couldn't bear the complete blackness outside when he looked out of his windows as his house was nowhere near any other lit-up place in the night-time dark. The long winter days were the worst, and on top of everything, he'd recently lost his wife, so his loneliness was even more marked.

He had recently enquired of his solicitors about selling the mansion and moving back to the city, but when they checked the official electronic property title register, they were astonished to find that it wasn't owned by Zooba at all, and so he had no right to sell it!

What the records showed was that he simply had a life interest in it under a trust which the prime minister had specially set up. This wasn't what he'd thought had been agreed to. He thought he owned it under the terms of their deal!

Zooba longed to be back in a three-bedroomed penthouse in the London suburbs like the one that he'd originally sold when he'd gone to live in the countryside, but prices had escalated so much because of the influx of foreign money that he soon found that he would now be lucky to get a one-bedroomed flat out in the sticks!

He had just decided to contact the Housing Ministry to see what could be done about it when he received a call from the prime minister's secretary inviting him up to London for discussions. Maybe, he thought, something useful was in the offing as he had kept his word and had given up all his anti-monarchy and anti–new law ambitions and activities as he'd promised, so he couldn't imagine anything but good coming out of such a meeting.

A flycar was sent for him, and he was filled with excitement on the journey that, after all this time, he might find himself being of service to his country in some way and his mind taken off his loneliness. On the journey, it dawned on him that he had certainly become a model citizen whilst growing older to be thinking that way about his country and no longer just about himself.

The flycar soon landed in Horse Guards Parade, just behind No. 10 Downing Street. This is where the ancient annual tradition of a military parade and remembrance still takes place in the presence of the monarch, watched all around the world.

Inside, the prime minister took him into a reception room, and they both sat down over a whisky to discuss matters. Zooba noticed that he was particularly friendly towards him and, feeling at ease, wondered what he was going to tell him.

The prime minister said, 'It's a while since we last met, Zooba, but between you and me—and I know you can keep a secret—we're still having endless trouble with alien beings. We thought that sending them off from the Sahara desert would be the last we would see of them, but others are still here. We're not even sure where they are any more. The Sahara being twenty times the size of Britain, they could even still be somewhere hiding in the desert, particularly as we know that they thrived on the heat there.

'We've sent coded messages around the world, asking for any reports of extraterrestrials, but so far, apart from one dubious report from Scotland, we only know of the ones who had been living in the museum and who then went off to go wherever they are now.'

'That is a very difficult problem,' Zooba said, 'but how do you think I can help?'

The prime minister replied, 'Well, you may well remember Yost. Have you had any communication with that being since you moved to the countryside? He might be helpful with our present predicament. We simply can't allow extraterrestrials to settle on Earth because Man would soon find himself evicted, if not extinct, before long.

'Do you still have the transponder that Yost gave you so you could still get in touch with each other? See what he can suggest.'

Zooba replied that he would be willing to do all he could to help. Yes, he'd kept the transponder as a memento but had no idea if it still worked.

'Well, I'll tell you what we'll do,' the prime minister said. 'You go back in one of the government's flytaxis and bring back the transponder so our technicians can check it over to ensure it is in full working order. There's no point setting off with it unless we're sure it works. You and I will then go up to our space station and try to get Yost's cooperation. How does that sound to you?'

Zooba replied, 'I'm very happy to cooperate, prime minister. I know it's not vital, nor do I want to trouble you over it, but there is another matter. Now that my wife's dead and I live all alone in the countryside, I dearly want to move back to London and buy a small place in one of its leafy suburbs. Do you think you could help me with this? I'd be nearer to things that way anyway.'

The prime minister now remembered why he hadn't given Zooba the country mansion outright but only a trust of a life interest. Of course, he said to himself, he had kept it as a future bargaining ploy if he ever needed Zooba's help again, and now the occasion had arisen.

So he said, 'Here's what I'll do, Zooba. You get Yost to help us, and I'll see to it that you can own a decent London house of your own and leave countryside living behind you once and for all.

'Indeed, on a temporary basis, I'd already planned for you to move into a vacant furnished bungalow we have in a north-west London suburb called Mill Hill, where I'm sure you'll be very comfortable.'

With that, he called in his assistant and asked him to arrange for Zooba to be moved back to London straight away with all his possessions, and it was not long before he found himself living once again with all the comforting, constantly light, and noisy surroundings of an overcrowded London suburb! He couldn't have been happier; it was music to his ears, and he was able to sleep like a log!

He was much nearer to where he needed to be to assist the prime minister and, in any case, had now been provided with his own personal flytaxi and driver.

CHAPTER FOUR

. . . . ●● ● ●● . . . .

The transponder turned out to be very difficult to fix. The engineers reported that as it had been created out in space, the materials making up its components were unobtainable on Earth, and they had needed to improvise with spare parts to make it work properly.

The main problem, they said, was its malfunctioning battery, but they had managed to install one of the latest lithium ion ones so that so far as they were concerned, it was now ready for intergalactic use.

They explained, in their report to the prime minister, that regular batteries didn't work as well out in the cold of space as the ones they normally used did. They'd tried it out and had sent messages on it to the International Space Station where they'd been received satisfactorily, but it remained to be seen whether, in its changed format, it was still compatible with the one Yost now had on the receiving end. He could well have upgraded his, they reported.

The prime minister realised that it was indeed possible that after all this time, Yost might well have updated his own model, making the two still incompatible, but all they could do when they got up there was to see what would happen when they sent him a message.

Arrangements were made for the prime minister and his close aide to go up to Zooba's old space station with him, and they soon arrived. It was still manned as it had been found quite useful for experimental space purposes to keep it so, and they soon settled in and went to sleep.

The next day, in the presence of the prime minister, Zooba sent a message to Yost, asking him to come to see him. At first, there was no response, hopefully because Yost was speaking to another alien on his transponder, but when Zooba tried again later, Yost answered. When he heard who it was, he uttered an unimaginable scream of delight to think that his old friend hadn't forgotten him and now wanted to see him.

Yost explained that he was far away on an experimental orbit and it wouldn't be for some days that he could get there, so it was arranged that as soon as he was near enough, he would let them know and he could come in.

Yost was actually having problems of his own and only said he was far away to give himself time to try to extricate himself from them. Other alien beings had found out, he knew not how, that he had aided Man to send them packing from the Sahara Desert with false threats of disease. They'd captured his spaceship with him in it and had made him their prisoner!

He was then made to man one of their spaceships as they had actually had some illness there, and he had eventually worked his way up to becoming its captain.

He waited for his chance, and soon after Zooba's call, he managed to steer it towards Zooba's location, fending off the other occupant of the spaceship in the process who was shouting that he thought they shouldn't be going in that abnormal direction as it was a dangerous course to take.

Nevertheless, he got there, and as soon as he arrived, he made his way across to Zooba's portal, and they let him in. He didn't look like his old self, Zooba thought, and he asked him how he had been since they'd last been together.

He couldn't restrain himself and told them the whole story of how he had been made a prisoner and had only been able to work himself up to the captain's position by pure chance, through another's illness. Otherwise, he would have been unable to come.

He went on, 'I've had a dreadful time since we last met. You cannot imagine what I've been through. I only told you about my being a prisoner in case they overheard me. You see, I found out that the alien being who hadn't been fooled by my scaremongering about Man's diseases had stayed behind and had left the Sahara and gone to live in a cave in a mountainside in the Alpes-Maritimes just across the Mediterranean in the south of France.

'He'd done what Early Man had done. He had found a rope ladder dangling down to the floor of the mountain and had climbed up it into the cave, drawing the ladder up after him. That way, he was quite secure and couldn't be got at. He must have taken French cheese with him, of course.

'Anyway, with his transponder, he'd communicated with the leader of the sect who was from a different tribe from his own. He was known as Quist. When he heard that there hadn't actually been any worldwide disease as I had pretended and that it was I who was responsible for their urgent departure from the desert, he was absolutely furious with me.

'He sent some of the others to waylay my spaceship, and it was towed, with me in it, to the main spaceship that Quist had for himself. I was afraid they'd destroy me, but instead, Quist was persuaded to put me on trial, and I was locked up in a cabin.

'He later came to my cabin and said quietly, so no one could hear him, that if I gave him some information which only I had, he would see to it that the charges would be dropped. I was in no position to argue but chanced my hand and said that I wanted the Pardon in advance.

'You remember, of course, that I designed the whole international security veil canopy around Earth and that we included a hatch which was securely guarded. Well, this was what he wanted to know about. He forced me to take him to it to reveal the special double-lock system I'd installed and to show him how it worked.

'The guards on duty there thought nothing of my showing someone around the installation as they knew me so well, so they didn't bother to report it, unfortunately for me as I might otherwise have been rescued by my people.

'Before he forced me back to his ship, I tried letting one of the guards who knew me what was going on, but for some reason, he didn't react and just smiled at me as we left.

'So there I was back in Quist's spaceship, wondering if he would keep his word and let me go. I hadn't actually revealed the whole secret of the hatch, however, because it needed a special code to open it up and I'd taken a great chance and given him a wrong one!

'Fortunately, he hadn't asked for a full demonstration as he was keen to get back for some reason. If he had, I would have had to give him the right code, and I'd worked out that I would have then pretended I'd made a mistake under pressure.

'He told me that he was pleased that he would now be in control of the hatch and everyone would pay him for access through it. Being happy with his achievement, he said I could now go back to my own spaceship, and no charges would be brought. But of course, if I did anything which he thought objectionable, I would certainly be brought before the Galaxy Court of Justice, and I should bear in mind that there are no time limits on bringing the serious charges which he would concoct.

'I played for time and asked him where this Galaxy Court was, and he said it used to be on Enceladus, one of the major inner satellites of Saturn. He said that when they'd discovered it, they'd found it to be an ocean-harbouring moon which enabled life to exist on its methane gases.

'He went on that they had intercepted messages that Man had worked out from probes that there was likely to be sufficient methane to support microbes in a form of life but that they hadn't realised that extraterrestrials were already living there and had developed underground cities within their own ecosystem.

'But all was not well because they had become overpopulated and the resources were insufficient to provide for everyone. This is why he said that they were searching for an alternative abode somewhere else in the galaxy, such as Earth.

'So you see why it took me some time to get here. My actions are probably being watched even now, so I can't stay long on my first visit, but I must get back soon and can then return, if necessary, much more secretly next time.'

Zooba thanked Yost for being so open with them and was sorry for all he'd been through. He said that they would keep the session short, but there was one thing he wanted to know—did Yost ever get the Pardon he had been promised?

Yost replied, 'If he had given it to me, I knew it wouldn't be worth anything because their documents were designed to disappear after twelve months, so they never had any written records after that. All arrangements were kept on their own version of the old Internet, so you never had anything you could take with you and actually show anyone.

'When I'd queried this practice as a youngster, I'd been told that space life wasn't compatible with written paper records because they were always short of storage space inside spaceships and their leader had opted for electronic records instead. I'd always wondered if this was true, especially now when I would have liked to be able to hold the Pardon safely in my hand.'

In response, the others told Yost that they were glad that he had overcome all his problems, and this put him at his ease.

CHAPTER FIVE

· · · · · · ●●● ● ●●● · · · · · ·

Zooba introduced the prime minister to Yost, who said he was honoured to meet him. The prime minister explained their predicament and asked if he could think how he could help. In return, he would do all he could to protect him from the others, but Yost would have to tell them how he thought this could be done.

Yost said he could see no reason why what he'd designed he couldn't redesign, particularly with regard to the all-important portal, and suggested that, when Quist wasn't about, they could go out further into space in the region of the Van Allen Belts and construct a new, secondary portal. 'It would work like how the old-time canal boats worked, where one had to go through consecutive locks to change the level of the water,' he said. 'So here, you would have to get past two portals instead of just one.'

The prime minister didn't waste time asking him how he knew about canal locks, but he did want to know why Yost thought that the Van Allen Belts would affect his plan.

Yost explained, 'The Van Allen Belts are high-energy radiation belts that contain a nearly impenetrable barrier that prevents electrons reaching the Earth. These charged particles are held in place by Earth's magnetic field, and the whole situation is constantly being studied so that scientists can predict when satellites are likely to be affected by radiation.

'It is understood that the inner belt stretches up to 6,000 miles above Earth's surface and the outer belt goes up 36,000 miles. We now understand that the space in between, called the plasmasphere, has virtually no electrons except when there is an unusually strong wind or a giant solar eruption, when the electrons from the outer belt can be pushed into it.

'So you can see that it is quite possible to construct our secondary portal, taking full account of what we know exists in outer space, and nothing can be done about it by Quist. We'll have to extend our veil outwards from where the first portal is so that it connects up with the area where the second one will be, but I can't see any problem doing that either. We'll work from a space platform which I'll construct.'

'What an amazing being you are,' the prime minister explained. 'You seem to have been following NASA's experiments in some detail to know all these facts. I think you have come up with the solution to our problem. Well done! So we'll now have double protection against unwanted visitors.'

Yost didn't let on how he had intercepted NASA's messages, which is why he knew so much about their experiments, and he was especially proud about what he'd learned from Quist about life on Enceladus.

CHAPTER SIX

· · · · · ·●●●● ● ●●●●● · · · · ·

Watching all the comings and goings and listening in to all the coded messages, Quist was ready for action. It was obvious that Yost was cheating on him by giving him the wrong code and continuing to help Zooba. He was certainly not going to let them install an extra portal, and if it meant a fight, then he wouldn't hesitate to have one.

Or, he then thought, why not instead let them install the double-portal system at their own expense? He could then take it over, control it himself, and collect all the dues from those using it. That would be much more sensible, he decided, and much less effort on his part until the time came when he could step in and take the combined system over for himself.

Quist, being very much disliked because he always put himself first, had his own enemies, and they too had learned all about the double-portal plan. He knew who they were from past experience, but if it came to it, he could muster more supporters than they could unless, of course, they all banded together, in which case he would be outnumbered. So secrecy was essential.

He knew from having dealt with them individually, however, that being from different sects, they kept themselves very much to themselves, and he didn't think they would ever combine to defeat him. Unless, of course, they were all threatened by some common disaster, which would be an entirely different matter. Very much like Man's constant predicament on Earth that he'd heard about, he imagined.

So he set about his new plan. Whilst Yost was on his way returning to his spaceship, Quist captured it, and when Yost got back and went inside, he was astonished to find Quist there waiting for him. He was told in no uncertain terms that if he valued his life, he would now prepare the double-portal system exclusively for Quist and not for Man.

He was now to pretend to do it as originally arranged so as to get the financial backing for the enterprise, he was told, but at the end of the work, he would hand over the codes to Quist and to no one else. If he didn't cooperate, he knew what would happen to him!

What choice did Yost have? If he refused and went against Quist's wishes, he knew what his fate would be. He knew what Quist was capable of as he had once witnessed at first hand Quist personally throwing one of their kind out into space with no protection, and that had been over some minor argument!

On the other hand, Yost had the upper hand because he alone knew the secret of how to construct the double-portal system, so he felt a bit happier over the whole situation on reflection.

Indeed, it was only through his connection with the prime minister that the necessary funds would become available for the whole project, but he decided to say none of this to Quist and to appear to go along with his orders, for the present at least. That seemed the sensible way forward, he thought.

CHAPTER SEVEN

· · · · · · ● · · · · · · · · ·

Yost told Quist that he thought it essential for him to get in touch with Zooba without delay as he would be wondering what had happened to him and that it would be sensible to get on with the double-portal construction before anyone tried to stop it going ahead.

Quist said, 'Take this as a final warning. You can go now and get it constructed, but if I find you've been double-crossing me over it, you know what will happen to you! There'll be nowhere to hide if I have to find you, so just bear this in mind.'

Yost quivered at this warning but thought that so long as he could now get out of Quist's clutches, there was always a way out of most situations. Nevertheless, he would bear this warning well in mind in the process.

He sent a message to Zooba that he wanted to see him again and was sorry he'd gone off without any message but that he couldn't help it. Zooba said he should come over to his ship so they could get on with the double-portal plan.

He was glad to get away from Quist and soon entered Zooba's spaceship. Zooba said that Quist should have known better than to think that his threats hadn't been overheard. They'd heard every word, and he wanted Yost to know that they would protect him during the construction process and that Quist would never get his hands on the finished product.

He then asked Yost what he needed in order to start the project, and he listed everything he had in mind when he had first thought up the double-portal system and a few other refinements which he'd thought of afterwards.

'Some of it would have to be put together out in space and the rest on Earth,' he said, explaining that outside of Earth's atmosphere, the necessary materials would have to be secured together very carefully indeed because of the different air pressure.

There would be solar storms and space debris to cope with whilst the work was carried out, but so far as any disruption by any aliens was concerned, he felt confident that they wouldn't cause any trouble.

'I know why that is,' Zooba said. 'We overheard Quist expecting everything to be completed and then him taking the whole thing over. Well, that's not how it's going to be. We will watch his activities closely, and at the end of the construction, we'll make sure we're in charge and not him.'

'We must now get down to pricing the project as we expect the whole world to chip in with their contributions, and we need to know what's involved.'

They discussed the different stages and costings necessary to accomplish their plan and came up with a figure which astounded them. How would they manage to raise such enormous amounts as hundreds of millions of dollars? they wondered.

Zooba said he'd better get back to see the prime minister about raising the finance and took the next flytaxi down to Earth, making an appointment on the way.

The prime minister asked if there was any way the costs could be reduced and suggested that the list that Yost had compiled with Zooba should be given to a space consultant whom he knew, to get his opinion.

Try as he could, the consultant could only chip away at a handful of items as the project was fraught with difficulties since it involved building out into deep space, requiring additional safety features for those working on it which would eventually be scrapped, such as the temporary working space platform, which would not be needed as part of the actual finished construction.

What the consultant did, however, was to compile a report on the project, and when he had received it by urgent messenger, the prime minister called a meeting of all the top world powers to discuss the project and its costings.

The meeting was scheduled to take place in the parliament buildings, but as he had done previously, he notified the delegates at the last minute that the venue had been changed to the BT Tower in case there were interceptors who knew about the original location and might cause trouble.

As had proved to be the case on previous similar occasions, some countries were willing to raise a precept on its people to contribute their share of the cost, whilst others pleaded economic pressures as to why they couldn't afford to join in.

The US president, who had come over specially for the meeting, told the delegates that, unless every country joined in as best it could, it was quite possible that extraterrestrials would inhabit the whole world. They knew, he warned, that there were some here already and it was essential that the double portal should be constructed without delay so they could be evicted. Meanwhile, they had to be found and locked up to prevent any trouble.

The delegates were told that they could contribute gradually during the construction process and that those who could demonstrate the necessary expertise could assist in the actual construction, giving employment to its citizens. And it was on that basis that the matter of finance was finally settled. Initial contributions were arranged to get the project going, and the meeting then broke up.

CHAPTER EIGHT

· · · · · · · ● · · · · · · · ·

Whilst all these events were going on, the aliens who had left the museum had been searching for a better place to establish themselves. They only moved about in the small hours so as not to be seen and, eventually finding themselves unable to discover any source of their essential cheese, ended up in the countryside, where they came across a cheesemaking factory by chance and broke in.

They were so hungry by then that they gorged themselves on the different cheeses, and by the time the staff came to open the factory next morning, they found the aliens all fast asleep on the floor of one of the rooms. Not flinching at finding sleeping aliens, the manager quickly locked them in and reported what he had found to the police.

All police stations had been asked to report to No. 10 Downing Street about any sightings of the elusive aliens, and it was not long before the prime minister was on the scene to see them for himself.

They were a motley-looking lot, he thought, and he was astonished when one of them spoke in perfect English to him, and said, 'Sir, we are here because we are lost. We want to return to our homeland but have no way of finding out how to get there. Our children are suffering by being taken from one place to another, and I am sure you would not like that to continue. Can you help us, please?'

The prime minister replied, 'We know one of your kind through one of our citizens. I will contact him straight away, and he will arrange things, but it must be understood that everyone must leave at the same time. We cannot have anyone left behind.'

The spokesperson assured the prime minister on that score, and contact was made with Zooba who arranged for Yost to meet them at the veil portal and let them out in a suitable space vehicle. They were flown up there, and Yost saw to the rest.

Afterwards, Zooba asked Yost where he thought they had returned to. He thought they couldn't just wander around in space, and Yost assured him that this wasn't the case, and said, 'You must have done some space research by now and heard about the Red Dwarfs. Well, there are planets surrounding a number of them on which life can be supported.'

He added, 'So far as I understand the research carried out by Man from their space telescopes, they can still only conjecture if life exists anywhere other than on Earth, but we extraterrestrials know the truth. You see, we know where it is possible for the right conditions to exist where our kind are able to live, and we have adapted to them. That is where they would have returned to.'

Yost reminded Zooba that much space exploration had taken place by Man, especially in the early part of the twenty-first century and then, subsequently, into the possibility of life on Mars and Jupiter.

Yost said, 'In the case of Mars, seasonal changes in methane levels had been recorded in its atmosphere sufficient to support life, and when Curiosity landed and examined its rocks, organic compounds were found, indicating the possibility of life being sustained there. But it was later found that the explorers came across cities of Martians who had no intention of letting them stay. So this is why further efforts were made, and Jupiter was found to be a far less hostile place, at least in theory, that is.

'As to Jupiter, the Juno spacecraft had captured time-lapse movies of it and of its moons, but afterwards, the scientists ran out of research money because of overpopulation, and Man had never been able to see through the clouds from so far away to see if life could actually be sustained there.

'So what Man never knew was that life did exist on both planets, and I am living proof! When Jupiter became the better place for us, we all moved there and took the Galaxy Court of Justice with us.

'The reason we all tried to leave to enter Earth was that we knew from our own experts that eventually, each Red Dwarf would become a Red Giant and be unable to maintain life any more. The same with Mars and Jupiter, we suspected.

'Just like Man has been searching space for alternative places to subsist when it might certainly become necessary at some time in the future, so extraterrestrials had the same object when landing on Earth. It will be touch and go if either lot succeed, but it will not be our worry because in both cases and so far as we know, there are many years of life conditions left there.

'There is no doubt, however, that these searches will continue for the sake of future generations, just to get ahead of the eventual catastrophe awaiting us all, when everything eventually collides and disintegrates.'

Zooba said he thought Yost was being too pessimistic and said so. There was still much to be discovered in the galaxy after all. He knew about the reason for the research Man was carrying out but had no idea that extraterrestrials had the same problem where they came from, searching for alternative living conditions.

He couldn't help commending extraterrestrials in general on their ability to adapt much better than Man seemed to have done so far, especially how they could converse in many different languages, which he thought gave them a definite advantage in their research.

· · · · · · · · · ● · · · · · · · · · ·

As the reports coming in at the BT Tower had only identified one other incursion, which was apparently outside Glasgow in Scotland, the prime minister sent Zooba to find out if they had discovered their whereabouts yet.

When he arrived, he went to see the Scottish First Minister by appointment to get the latest information. It turned out that the aliens had disappeared since the first sightings had been reported, so Zooba mentioned what they had found out about their liking for cheese.

Hearing this, the First Minister immediately got his aide to check around the cheese shops in case there had been any unusual activity, and sure enough, one of them had been broken into quite recently and the stock partly eaten, with bits left around on the floor and the rest mostly removed from the place.

Detectives were brought in, and the aliens were eventually tracked down in a warehouse. Zooba informed Yost about it, and it was not long before they were all duly despatched from Earth through Yost's portal.

So far as was known, therefore, all aliens had finally been removed from Britain, and no others had since been reported. So a great sigh of relief went up from a grateful population.

Further checks were routinely made around the world for any sightings, but all seemed quiet for the present.

CHAPTER NINE

· · · · · · · ●● ● ●● · · · · · ·

Two alien beings had secretly separated themselves from the main group in London when the others had been rounded up and sent back. In appearance, they were much stronger than the others. It must have been something in their genes, but either way, they were able to adopt the guise of human beings. Their strength enabled them to breathe without any equipment, and for all anyone knew, they were the same human species as Man in appearance.

This ability to transform themselves was a great advantage as they had decided that they were not going back, to be left possibly wandering around in space from one place to another, when Earth seemed a very suitable place to live, at least for the time being.

They expected to be found out any moment, but the longer they stayed and conversed with humans, the more they got to know their ways and manner of speaking. And after just a few years, you couldn't tell the difference.

In their early days on Earth, people did wonder about their idiosyncrasies, but they learned from their mistakes and copied everything they saw and heard, eventually making them virtually indistinguishable from the crowd.

One day, they were wandering around the streets of London looking for somewhere to live, and they came across a hostel run by a charity where they stayed until they came across somewhere of their own.

Naturally, they didn't know anything about Man's money laundering rules, which were an obstacle to buying a property because they insisted on one producing acceptable identification, which they didn't have. And they soon discovered that the only alternative was to rent. And even that wasn't possible as they had no money!

Continuing to stay therefore in the hostel, they wandered around the streets and eventually came across a courthouse where the public are always allowed to go in and watch the proceedings, but they didn't know this.

As it began raining heavily, they went in for shelter. Walking to the seats at the back, nobody seemed troubled by their appearance. They just thought they might be there as family of witnesses in a case.

They then noticed the body of a judgebot on display in a cabinet, looking very sorry for itself. They knew a great deal about robots where they had come from and wondered if they could somehow make money from this judgebot, as it said it was called on the notice.

So when the court proceedings finished for the day, they hid themselves so that the ushers didn't see them when they locked up, and this gave them the chance to break into the cabinet and take the judgebot out.

It was clearly intended to have once been used in place of human judges as it was so cleverly designed, but what intrigued them more was, as they examined it more closely, that it was capable of being monitored remotely. It must have gone out of use; hence it was lying in the cabinet. So they inserted one of the power chargers they always kept on them, and sure enough, it seemed to come to life, ready to obey their instructions!

They struck on the idea of taking it back to Jupiter where the Galaxy Court of Justice was now held, with the intention of getting financial backing to reproduce a number of them and to install them in place of judges, explaining to their officials that this system would be much cheaper to run than real alien judges. Then they could make their fortune by controlling court outcomes remotely in return for suitable large rewards.

There was only one major problem. Without money, how could they get back to Jupiter and, indeed, how to get the judgebot out with them as well?

· · · · · · · · ● · · · · · · · · · ·

By this time, there were regular flytaxis from Britain to various destinations in space where spacecraft and space stations were in orbit, and the pair decided to rob some people of enough money to pay for the fare, the idea being that once out in space, they would take over the vehicle and take themselves to Jupiter with the judgebot.

Watching other pickpockets go about their trade, they soon found that sliding their slim hands into pockets soon produced enough money for their journey without being discovered, and they were soon on their way. Hostel life had been all very well, but they couldn't wait to get back to their Jupiter homeland and make their fortune. How glad they were that they had stayed behind!

They'd heard how other planets had become ravaged by severe climate change which had led to fighting, annexation of land, and disease, with large swathes becoming uninhabitable and the complete loss of the rule of law. But Jupiter had so far avoided most of these calamities.

But even there, the climate was gradually becoming intolerably cold, and frequent voyages from there around the galaxy had become common, searching for sanctuary.

It should be explained that although credit cards had, at one stage, virtually replaced the use of cash, the fact was that by this time, people had lost their trust in them because their accounts had frequently become accessed by criminals. And they had reverted back to cash kept in pockets, which is how the pair had managed to pay for their transit back to Jupiter.

CHAPTER TEN

· · · · · ·●●●●●●●● · · · · · · ·

In those days, it was still a lengthy journey to get there, and they found themselves occupying themselves with tales about the oddities of human beings, wondering how they would manage to live side by side with them if it ever came to it.

One of them, called Reko, said that from what he had already seen on Earth, he was surprised that he'd noticed that Man gradually became infirm and ill before dying, whereas they never did. Somehow, it was normal for his own kind to live their life fully with all their faculties intact until they suddenly died peacefully in their sleep and, even then, always at a great age.

He said he'd noticed that some of the older humans had difficulty seeing and others hard of hearing, whilst others used wheelchairs to get about. And that was apart from those who'd become so forgetful that they had to be kept in a special place because of their cognitive disability. He wondered if this would happen to them if they ever had to go to live on Earth and ever intermixed with humans. It was certainly a possibility.

The other being, called Marky, said that he'd noticed the same difference and thought it must have something to do with their genes, which he'd learned about in school.

Marky went on to say that he couldn't believe that Man actually joked about his feebleness in old age but that he'd heard two men recounting some humorous stories when he'd stopped at a street corner for breath.

'Oh, go on,' Reko said, 'can you remember any? We've got plenty of time until we arrive.'

Marky said he remembered a couple, and went on, 'A famous singer decided he'd do some charity work for free and went along to a retirement home for old people, where he gave a recital. Although he was well known generally, these residents didn't have particularly good memories, and so when he'd finished, there was very little applause.

'He was quite distressed by this as he'd expected them to be delighted with his performance, so he went up to a little old lady and said, "Have you any idea who I am?"

'She looked back at him in a concerned way and said, "Don't worry, my dear. Matron will tell you!"'

Reko was beside himself with laughter, although when he'd settled down, he felt sorry for her.

He then asked Marky, 'So what was the other joke you overheard?'

Marky said, 'There was an old couple in a restaurant who, as they always did, ordered exactly the same courses. Indeed, they shared everything. An old friend spotted them and came over and was asked to join them.

'During their conversation, he noticed that although the man was already eating, his wife hadn't even started. Intrigued by this, he asked the wife why she hadn't started, and she replied, "Oh, that's because I'm waiting until he's finished with the teeth we share between us!"'

This was too much for Reko, and he laughed his head off. Marky then said that he'd heard one more, and it went like this:

'A volunteer in an old peoples' home thought that to pass the time, he would try some simple arithmetic on the residents to keep their brains alert, so he asked one of them what two times two comes to. The answer soon came back, "Wednesday".

'He then asked the other one at the table what two times two makes, and she said "700".

'In desperation, he asked the third person the same question and was delighted that he got the answer right: "Four".

'"That's very clever. How did you do it?" he asked him.

'"Oh, that's easy" came the reply. "I simply deducted Wednesday from 700"'!

Every time they thought about these human jokes, they burst out laughing, but Marky pointed out that they just showed how frail Man gets when he's old and that if they ever had to come to live on Earth, he hoped they wouldn't have to suffer the same way.

When they finally landed, they found Quist waiting for them. He too had found Jupiter to be the most likely to last longer than the other planets and had set up home there with his family in the largest township near the space airport.

Through his connections, he'd heard that the two were coming back with something very interesting and couldn't wait to find out what it was.

As soon as he saw them, he wanted to know what they had brought. Quist was well known for being an entrepreneur amongst alien beings, and in the order of things there, he was quite an important figure.

The two, Reko and Marky, had no choice but to unwrap the judgebot, and upon seeing it, Quist realised immediately the potential it had for making money.

Being the crafty character he was, Quist suggested that they might like to use his factory's facilities for duplicating them, and once they'd got the idea off the ground, he promised he would share the spoils with them as equal partners.

Legal matters on Jupiter were not the same as in Britain, as you might expect. Formal arrangements were documented verbally on computers instead of on paper, and so this arrangement was recorded that way as well. In this way, it made things simpler if a dispute came before the Galaxy Court of Justice.

But Quist had found a way of getting into this contract system surreptitiously and altering words, giving them different meanings in his favour whenever he got involved in court cases, and so he always won! Nobody had ever tumbled to the fact that he'd altered the evidence— they just thought it had been recorded wrongly—but, nevertheless, could never understand how he managed to succeed every time he was sued!

Just as their airtaxi was making its approach to the landing platform, another one, also planning to land, came too near to them and caught one of their main antennae, breaking it off.

Suddenly, they found their guidance screens had gone blank. They couldn't stop in mid flight to replace it, so their pilot was forced to use his lengthy experience and peer out of a forward window to judge the right course to take.

Other flying vehicles almost hit them too as they came in to land, but somehow, they were fortunate enough to avoid everything around them and finally landed.

They were quite shaken up by these near misses but didn't take too long to recover once they were there.

CHAPTER ELEVEN

· · · · · ·●●●●●●●●●●●●● · ·

Q uist had already forced Yost to show him how the double lock was going to work once the extension to the protective veil had been installed, albeit that Yost had given him the wrong code to open it.

There was no way he could test the code until the extension was in place, so he had to wait until then anyway. But once that had happened, he could control who passed through and charge each of them a hefty toll for the privilege.

Meanwhile, here was yet another opportunity opening up which could be very lucrative indeed and more immediate.

Once the judgebots had been installed in the Galaxy Court of Justice, he could make it known in the underworld that in return for suitable recompense, he would ensure that lighter sentences would be passed on criminals or, if he was given sufficient, he would get them off entirely on some legal pretext or other.

This was very similar to what they had been used to on Earth until the authorities had discovered what was going on and had banned their use, but on Jupiter, he could see himself cashing in long before anyone realised what was happening under their very noses.

He could now see himself retiring with enough to be able to forget all about his plans about taking over the double-lock system from Man.

As Reko and Marky went into the arrival lounge, Quist suggested that they should expand on the plans for their partnership over the judgebots, and they sat in a corner talking quietly so nobody could hear.

Quist said, 'I know you must be tired from your journey, especially the fright you must have had with those near misses. As I see it, whilst the seven judgebots are being created, we have to find a way to get the authorities to want to replace our normal judges, and I have an idea.

'We'll spread it around, as already seems to be the case from what I've heard, that the judges want even more and more money to sit in the Galaxy Court of Justice, and we can then come forward with our much cheaper alternative—our judgebots. There will be no charge for supplying and installing them in the court, with lifetime guarantees, and I suspect that the authorities will jump at the opportunity to economise that way.

'There are already rumblings about the decline in the economy and shortages, although fortunately, as our beings live healthy lives until we die, our hospitals are very much emptier than on Earth, and we need far fewer of them.

'Also, I have a few friends on the committee that appoint the judges, so I reckon that if I let them in on the idea, they'll cooperate with our plans. On the other hand, if I can get their cooperation without bringing them in on it and rewarding them, then of course, there will be more for us to share out.

'We must also make sure that when the judgebots have been created, they contain the right electronics so that they can be controlled from my central depot, and I suggest that one of us should take one into the back of the court to check this out and make sure that our signals can reach in there.

'There is always the possibility that the building has been constructed in such a way as to repel outside signals from getting in. So this is very important. We don't have to take the whole body in, just the head, so no one should notice what we're doing.'

· · · · · · · · · ● · · · · · · · · · · ·

At that moment, one of the members of the judges' appointments committee happened to have arrived back from a trip and spotted his friend Quist in the corner of the spaceport. He said he'd had a difficult journey because Man was experimenting with flights near Jupiter and had nearly caused them to crash.

Quist said they'd had a similar problem. He decided he had no intention of broaching his plan at this early stage, especially as he hadn't even got his plans off the ground, so he just chatted with him, just to renew their friendship.

The friend said he had some time to kill until his local connection took off and that he'd heard of a remarkable story from one of their judges at a gathering they'd had, and he unfolded the story:

'A criminal was before the court for damage to property. Soon after, he'd been released from prison. He was a scrounger and previously happened to be in the prison hospital with another two, one of whom was very old.

'It came out that the two wanted to play a trick on him in reprisal for his having taken some valuables from the old one during the night. So they concocted the following plan.

'The old one leaned over to his friend and passed a piece of paper, whispering, but in earshot of the scrounger, that it was a map showing where he had stashed his loot after a robbery and that he was to have it if he died.

'Next day, one of their prison pals came round with a trolley of books and, by arrangement, slipped the map into one of them for safekeeping and left. The scrounger noticed this and went to the pal's cell afterwards, threateningly asking for the map. He was told that if he handed over the old one's valuables, he could have it.

'Thinking he would do better with the map of where the loot was than with the old one's trinkets, the exchange took place, and the old man got his possessions back.

'Being released a couple of days later, the scrounger waited until night-time and, having found the place where the map showed the stash to be, started digging.

'Suddenly, several lights came on, and he was revealed digging up a judge's front garden, for that was where the map showed the stash to be!

'You can imagine the rest. Security agents protecting the judge's property soon secured him, and he was back in prison like a shot for intentional criminal damage, and as we have heard, the old one got his valuables back!

'They all thought that to be a remarkable story and how cleverly they'd got their own back on the scrounger for having stolen the old man's precious valuables in the first place.'

CHAPTER TWELVE

· · · · · · · · ● ● · · · · · · · · · ·

Much remained to be done to get Quist's scheme off the ground. Manufacturing and then testing these judge robots were the easier parts. Persuading the authorities to use them was much more difficult. And then an extraordinary event occurred.

A group of extraterrestrials had just forced their way in from a neighbouring planet, and after some difficult detective work, they were identified, charged, and put on trial. This had put a much extra burden on the court's systems, and Quist's friend happened to meet up with him again at a conference and told him of the problem.

They couldn't delay dealing with the invaders' cases because their countrymen might well arrive in force, which is the last thing they wanted. Nor could they just send them back to Jupiter without trial because it would give the wrong message about their justice system, not only locally but out in other planets as well.

If they were tried and deported, that would be best, they thought. But the court had a backlog of cases because some judges had been ill from some infectious disease, and others had been on strike for more pay, so they were in quite a quandary.

This was Quist's opportunity to propose installing the judgebots. His friend thought that here was the solution to the problem when Quist told him of his plan, and Quist, in turn, was delighted to see that the idea was going to sell itself without any bribes having to be paid simply because of the urgency of finding a solution to the current shortage of judges in the Galaxy Court of Justice.

The checks on whether remote messages sent into the judgebots' heads inside the court building had turned out to be more than satisfactory, so the authorities felt confident enough to announce that they'd had enough of the judges' constant demands and complaints and were going to replace the whole lot of them with robot judges who would cost their population nothing once they were up and running.

This proved to be a popular move as anything to save the populace money was always certain to go down well politically.

At first, the court officials found it difficult to get on with these strange beings but soon realised that their use was actually making their work much easier. Of course, there was no sign at all that every judgement was being controlled remotely from Quist's lair by other robots, which he had programmed rather cleverly to deliver the right result in each case, according to the extent of the bribes that had been paid.

The word soon went around the underworld that if they remunerated Quist appropriately, the criminals could be sure of being dealt with leniently, and he soon became well known for it.

But this bonanza couldn't last long because the criminals realised that they were too much in his hands, and they had to do something about it. They didn't want to stop the system because it was so valuable, so they did the next best thing.

They organised a meeting of the gang leaders in the headquarters of the one who was well known for drug running, and they discussed the problem at length.

In the end, they decided that they did indeed want to run it for themselves, and so long as the authorities were happy with judgebots instead of real judges, all the criminal gangs, or at least those who had been allowed in on it, could save themselves a great deal of bribery money.

They got together a small group who waylaid Quist one evening and killed him. The way was now clear for them to benefit solely from the judgebot scheme, except for one thing. They didn't know how to programme the judgebots for their own benefit, and until they did, they would operate normally without any interference from the criminals!

CHAPTER THIRTEEN

· · · · · ● ● ● ● ● ● ● · · · · · · ·

B ack on Earth, the prime minister urgently called another meeting of his PMG group because there had just been another incursion from space, but this time, it was much more serious.

It had occurred in Washington DC, and he'd had a call on the hotline from the US president telling him that a number of extraterrestrials had occupied the Capitol building in large numbers, where Congress meets. He had heard, of course, of Zooba's friend Yost, and he wondered if there was any way that Zooba could contact him and get him to intervene with them to persuade them to leave. Otherwise, he said, the alternative was too gruesome to contemplate.

The National Guard were quite able to deal with them on their own, but he felt that if Yost could intervene and, in his way and knowing how they think, get them to depart peacefully, it could be better in the long run that way.

The prime minister reminded the president that assuming they had the same habits as the ones they'd had in London, cheese was their sole source of food. The president replied that even if that was still the case with this lot, there was ample cheese in the Capitol's kitchens for them to be getting on with.

Obviously, it wouldn't last forever, but he would like to get shot of them at the earliest opportunity as they were completely disrupting the day-to-day affairs of state.

He told the prime minister that the normal meetings were now being held in the White House for the present, but the main worry was that all their working papers and computers were now in the aliens' hands, so if he could act quickly, it would be much appreciated.

The prime minister said he would do his utmost to help resolve the situation since he realised it could well affect the security of the whole world if it were allowed to get out of hand any further.

He contacted Zooba, telling him what had occurred, and asked him if he could get Yost to intervene as quickly as possible as the situation was most serious.

As ever, Yost was most helpful, especially where his friend Zooba was concerned, and he landed down in Washington to confront the others.

When he went in, he was astonished at how many there were. They'd uprooted the place searching for food until they'd finally found the kitchens and raided the fridges of all the cheese supplies.

He sought out their leader and was very surprised to discover that it was none other than Quist himself. Although his killers had left him for dead, he had survived the attack and recovered because of his natural alien resilience.

Apparently, the aliens had been getting quite fractious back in Jupiter, wanting to find a safer long-term place to live, and they had approached him to help lead them to a suitable place on Earth. Naturally, he was happy to oblige in return for payment for each individual!

Quist told him that things hadn't been great for him for some time. The aliens had somehow found out that he had promoted himself to a position where he was all supreme and was ordering them about until, one day, three of them had waylaid him and effectively made him their prisoner, demanding that he showed them the way through the portal.

His life depended on him helping them through it, but when they all arrived there and it came to entering the secret code Yost had given him, it failed to budge. He tried different codes haphazardly, hoping against hope that one of them would open it, but to no avail.

However, for some strange reason after the electronics had reverted to their default position, the portal opened of its own accord, and they all got through, and he was suddenly off the hook.

Quist had previously told them all about the food problem and diseases on Earth, but they just wouldn't listen and were adamant that they intended to carry out their plan to occupy Earth, whatever the consequences.

So for his own protection, he decided to bring them all to Washington where he knew they couldn't last long anyway since the National Guard would soon dispose of them.

The Guard's motto was 'Always ready, always there', he'd heard somewhere, and their assistance could soon be brought in to help if all else failed.

The problem with the food idea was that the aliens who had been living on Earth for a while had discovered that, after all, their bodies were able to tolerate some of the other food that Man used. Other milk products, such as butter, yoghurt, and the milk itself, were found to be tolerated, and in the end, the Congress kitchens were found to be devoid of those items as well!

· · · · · · · · · ● · ● · · · · · · · · · ·

When Yost went inside and spoke to Quist privately, he asked him how they had got into the Capitol. After all, he said, the place was regularly locked up. Quist said that their slim bodies easily fitted into the ventilation ducts, and that's how they did it. They'd got in beside the Exhibition Hall, where the pipes went, and had settled there amongst the exhibits.

They'd also got lost inside the Metro system before that, he added. Apparently, they'd come across the Union entrance on Massachusetts Avenue and had gone right round the whole train system until they'd been chased out by some vigilant passengers who'd unusually raised their eyes from their newspapers and chased them out into the street where a passing cop gave chase but somehow lost them in the crowd, as they were so nimble.

Yost explained that America had recently gone through a period of overpopulation and that, as a consequence, resources such as food were scarce. In the early part of the twenty-first century, the policy was to exclude so many foreigners to keep down numbers, he said, that they had found themselves short of skilled labour. And under the new president, the policy of strict border controls was reversed, with the result that with too many foreigners having been allowed in and not all being skilled, they were using up all the country's resources without contributing to the taxes. This meant that now there certainly wasn't enough to sustain the incomers from space as well.

What a liar he was when he wanted to be! There was no such problem with the economy or the country's resources, as the current president was doing an excellent job in controlling immigration, limiting it to just those and their families, who could prove that they had the useful skills that the country needed.

· · · · · · · · ● · · · · · · · · · · ·

Quist, now having regained his authority, began to plan how to persuade the others that any expedition into Earth was not going to be successful, and he called together the elders of the group and explained that they ought to leave for their own sakes.

A gathering in the main meeting chamber was organised, and everyone was told the situation and that they were to wait for their friend Yost to arrange safe passage back into space.

Yost then left the meeting to go, by arrangement, to see the president who said he would prefer them to leave peacefully rather than by force. He signed a presidential executive order that they should be given safe conduct from the country.

The head of the National Guard was amazed when he went into the Congress building to organise their departure pursuant to the executive order and saw actual alien beings, which he had only seen depicted in films. They were nothing like those he'd seen in the cinema and in books. Indeed, he thought they were rather charming beings.

He felt that so long as they cooperated peacefully, they could be escorted outside and taken to the nearest spaceport without any harm coming to them. He organised quantities of their types of food to be provided, which they took with them.

Making sure that their numbers were known exactly was one of his priorities, and he arranged for them to be lined up to register. He decided that checking them by name was going to be fruitless because their names were so abnormal, so he arranged for a designated number to be permanently attached to each individual so they could be checked easily on the journey.

Whilst this was being seen to, two of their number decided that they didn't want to leave. And being at the back, they slipped away without being seen and certainly not given a permanent number on their arms.

They crept into a nearby park and sat in the fork of some tree branches, wondering how to make a go of existing in this very strange environment called Earth.

The rest of the group obeyed orders and were conveyed back out through the portal, telling Yost that they would be making for Jupiter to rethink their plans.

He promised their leader that if he ever found a better alternative than Jupiter, he would come and help them to get to it. He reminded him that changes were constantly taking place within the galaxy and a better, longer-lasting planet could well present itself for them to occupy before they all eventually perished on Jupiter.

CHAPTER FOURTEEN

The two escapees eventually made their way out of Washington, walking mostly in the dark, not to be seen, and ended up in another woods.

Sitting in a tree, they spotted some smoke rising up from the ground, and they went to investigate. Maybe there was something useful there. One of them, named Bec, was female, and the other, called Jon, was the male member of the pair.

As they traced the source of the smoke, they came across a campfire which they approached cautiously as they had never seen smoke or fire before. Some bodies were lying around the fire, wrapped up in sleeping bags, but they couldn't tell whether there were humans inside or not. Either way, they were not particularly concerned as they didn't intend to disturb them, just wanting to take what they thought could be useful.

They found a spare sleeping bag which they planned to occupy together as they were so slim, and they came across the food store in a bag from which they quietly took what they thought useful.

One of the occupants stirred whilst they were gathering things up, having heard something, but soon fell asleep again. The man who was supposed to be on night duty whilst the others slept had himself fallen asleep so that, having taken all they wanted, they were able to make themselves scarce without disturbing the others and settled down in another part of the woods for the remainder of the night.

· · · · · · · · · · ● ● ● ● ● ● · · · · · · · · ·

When the aliens were being lined up and given out their numbers, a couple of them were heard talking, and it appeared that they had noticed the disappearance of Bec and Jon. This conversation happened to be overheard by Yost, and he reported it to his friend Zooba. Members of the National Guard were put on notice, and a search party was put together to seek them out.

They knew that they couldn't have gone far, so at first light, the search party was despatched to find them. It never occurred to them that they might be up in the trees, which is why although they passed under them twice, they didn't discover them! They searched cottages in the woods, outhouses, and barns without success and reported back for further orders.

Bec and Jon thought this was great fun. The soldiers had got so close and hadn't seen them!

The search was called off mid-morning as the officer in charge decided there was no point running around in circles, leaving it for another group to join the search later on in the day.

The couple came down from the tree they'd spent the night in, once they saw the soldiers make off, and went in search of food. They were also feeling the early morning cold as they'd been used to constant warm weather back in Jupiter.

Just as they thought they'd made a terrible mistake separating from the others, they came across a deserted cottage and went in through the open door. It had things on the walls as they went into each room and, by pressing them, found that lights came on each time they did it.

They'd never seen this sort of thing before and were intrigued how it happened each time they did it. They didn't know where the power came from, and perhaps it was just as well, as they might have electrocuted themselves investigating it!

Suddenly, the front door opened, and in came a man. He was obviously the owner of the cottage, judging by his furious demeanour when he saw them.

'What on earth are you doing in my cottage, and who are you anyway?' he demanded, taking in their very strange appearance.

He was quite taken aback suddenly seeing these strange beings. He'd read about extraterrestrials but thought that it was all just imaginary fiction written and filmed to excite people about the possibility of their existence. And yet here were two of them in his very own cottage!

He'd asked his question without thinking that they might not know Man's language and was astonished when he received the following reply from Jon: 'Sir, we have come from Jupiter with a large group but got separated from them by mistake. We're not sure if we can survive on Earth on our own as everything is so strange. Can you help us? We mean you no harm, and we'd like to stay if possible, as Jupiter has only so long left before it disintegrates into a black hole, destroying everything in the process.'

The man, called Joe, couldn't help taking pity on these frail-looking creatures, so he said, 'Are there any more of your kind roaming around? I need to know because you might be discovered if the authorities search for them.'

Bec replied, 'They've already been looking for us but hopefully have called off the search.'

Joe had become very lonely once his wife had died and, in a strange way, took to these two, somehow feeling they could give him a renewed interest in life. He'd have to find a way of concealing them from the outside world, but his cottage was in a remote part of the woods anyway and people rarely came that way.

Joe asked them to show him if they had any weapons, and they produced a couple of knives and transponders which he said he would lock up so he could sleep soundly in his bed at night and that, on that basis, they could stay and help him on the smallholding attached to his cottage.

Bec said, 'You don't know what a relief it is, your agreeing to take us in like this. We know we look unusual, but maybe we can get hold of some human clothes to make us look better for you.'

Joe replied, 'Oh, that's not important. What matters is that you both behave yourselves and make yourselves useful about the place. I'm getting older, and an extra pair of hands will be very helpful. Funnily enough, you seem to have come along at exactly the right time.'

He went on, 'Tell me, I always thought that Mars was where Man hoped to settle as an alternative to Earth, but you say you come from Jupiter. Why did this change happen?'

He was a simple soul and really didn't know one planet from the other. He was quite contented in his humble way to leave things like that to the experts and get on with his life scraping an existence in the forest.

'Well, you see, it was the same for our kind,' Bec answered. 'Our ancestors came from Uranus, which eventually became unstable, and they settled in Mars, which then did the same. Jupiter became the best alternative after that, so if Man still hopes to settle on Mars, he'll have a big surprise when he arrives!'

At that moment, they heard the sound of footsteps, and a soldier banged loudly on the front door. Joe went to answer it and found a soldier on the front step who said they were searching for two extraterrestrials who had escaped from the main party and that he had been designated to check every dwelling in that segment of the forest.

He said his orders were to enter everywhere to seek them out and that it was just as much for their sake that this was being done because they didn't have the means for survival on Earth. They had to be sent back anyway, he said, as we can't have them colonising Earth when Man is so pressed for space there already.

Whilst this discussion was going on, and before Joe let him in, Bec and Jon hid themselves by squeezing into a broom cupboard and hiding behind some of Joe's old clothes he kept there.

The soldier had been tipped off when instructions were given that extraterrestrials are very slim and can hide in the smallest of places, so his search was very thorough, and it was not long before he discovered them in there. He dragged them out, but just as he'd got them out in the open, Joe crept up behind him and smothered him with a heavy cloth which he usually used to keep warm in the Winter.

Between the three of them, they disarmed him and tied him up in a chair. Although he struggled, he couldn't extricate himself.

He said, 'You know you're wasting your time doing this to me. My comrades will soon miss me, and there will be the biggest search party ever seen sent to find me.'

Joe replied that he liked the aliens and that he intended to look after them as part of his family, and they could help him in his old age. They would do no harm to anyone and ate very little anyway, so what was the problem with that?

The soldier scratched his head and said that he'd been told that alien beings carried diseases from outer space and that if they were to spread, Man's constitution would have no way to resist it, having no known treatment. And they would fall like flies, and Earth would be taken over by aliens. He asked him if that's what he wanted.

He said he was told it would take only one alien to spread their diseases, so he was honour-bound to find every possible way to take them in for return to Jupiter.

Joe tried another tack. Bec and Jon had told him how they were able to make themselves disappear, and he said so. He didn't add, as they had done, that it was a gift they were born with but could only be used three times in their lifetime so had to be used sparingly and only when life-and-death occasions occurred.

The soldier said, 'All right then. Show me how you do it.'

Bec replied, thinking quickly, 'We can only do it out in the open, and we're certainly not going to let you free to come out and see.'

The soldier thought to himself that his best bet was to go along with things in the hope that he would soon be missed and the normal protocol put in hand to send out a search party to find him. He said that he would cooperate with their plans and not cause any trouble, which put their minds at rest.

Bec and Jon had another trick up their sleeves. They had been taught how to make a building seem to disappear! Unlike the limit placed on using the disappearance capability for their personal bodies, this could be used only once in their lifetime. What strange abilities these aliens had!

After discussing the situation carefully, they decided that this was the time to use it, and as a result, the cottage mysteriously disappeared from sight. No search party would be able to find it, and their location would remain a secret.

The trouble was, however, that no account had been taken of the smoke from the building's fire. Fire and smoke were unknown to the extraterrestrials as had already been revealed, so when the disappearance ability had been devised in Jupiter, no account was taken of it.

Consequently, when the search party arrived on the scene, having seen the smoke appearing as if by magic from where a chimney would have been, they soon realised that some trick had made the building disappear.

They banged on the place where they thought the door would be, but there was no answer. So they got hold of a long ladder lying on the ground, and one of them found an open window by feeling up and down the wall and entered inside. He crept quietly down the stairs and confronted the group with his firearm. Bec and Jon looked at each other in amazement that someone had got in. In a moment, they'd made themselves disappear from sight, just leaving Joe and the soldier visible.

He let the others in, and they untied the soldier and asked him what had happened. He recounted the whole episode, looking round pointlessly for the aliens to prove his point and, not seeing them, said they must have escaped.

Hearing this, they ignored the old man who had helped to tie the soldier up since arresting him and taking him with them would hold them up unnecessarily as he wouldn't be able to keep up with the chase to find the aliens. So they just said they would come back and see to him later.

The moment that they'd all left with the soldier and the cottage still being invisible, Joe put out the fire and went upstairs to shut the window. Fortunately, it was warmer weather once again, and they didn't need the fire or the open window. What would happen if it turned colder remained to be seen.

Reports were received that the extraterrestrials had disappeared and couldn't be found, so the search was finally called off. So long as Joe kept their secret about the invisibility capability, they could stay with him, and for his part, he was happy to have their company and help him about the place.

CHAPTER FIFTEEN

· · · · · · ●● ● ●● · · · · · · ·

By this time, Bec and Jon had become very close friends, and one night, they went about creating a baby alien. It was not done in the human way but just needed very close friendship and a joint willingness to achieve it.

Next morning, they presented their baby to Joe, who said he was amazed how tiny its hands and feet were. But trouble was brewing because alien babies always cry all day and night. And Joe, valuing his normal unbroken sleep, said that he was very sorry, but now that they had a baby, he couldn't tolerate the noise and, regretfully, was obliged to ask them to leave as soon as possible.

The couple hadn't expected this result because they'd grown up with babies crying all the time and thought it to be normal.

Jon said that maybe they could use their invisibility trick again, but Bec was reluctant to waste their second of three invisible tricks and would prefer to leave the place. In any case, she said, the baby wouldn't be invisible even if they used it up for themselves, pointing out that they'd been warned that the invisibility capability only applied to babies over one year old, and the baby would still be heard even if she was invisible.

Jon said she was right of course, and for the sake of their baby, they would have to leave, which they did. Joe was unhappy that he was alone again, but at least in his old age, he could sleep at night!

The invisibility of his cottage gradually wore off, piece by piece. He was outside when he saw the top half of his front wall appear again, followed by a window in another wall, and so on. It was like a jigsaw puzzle gradually completing itself and was quite eerie to watch.

It was sad because it meant that he couldn't stay there any more because the soldiers said they'd come back for him. He gathered together a few essentials and left, locking the place up. He put the cottage on the market, which would enable him to buy another place once sold. He arranged for his possessions to be placed in storage in the meantime and gave the keys to the agent.

It was not long before a young couple snapped up his charming cottage in the woods, and he was able to hide from the authorities in his new home in a different district.

As for the alien couple with their newborn baby, they didn't have much choice but to find their way back to Jupiter. That was easier said than done because everywhere they went, the baby's constant crying made people only too keen to get away from them and point them out.

They'd picked up a few of Joe's valuables without his knowledge when living in his cottage, and by turning them into money, this paid for their passage home. They realised that they'd not been very honest with him but saw it as the only way to safeguard the baby as well as themselves, of course.

They eventually got back in one piece and regretted having left the main party when they'd all gone back to Jupiter without them.

CHAPTER SIXTEEN

· · · · · · ●●● ● ●●● · · · · · ·

Back in the Galaxy Court of Justice on Jupiter, the judgebots were starting to develop mechanical problems. Serious criminals were being let off with short or no sentences, and the others were being sent down for long stretches. This simply couldn't be allowed to continue, the authorities realised.

Quist was called back in and did his best to repair the faults, but the electronic wizardry involved proved to be beyond his capabilities. Experts in that field had gone off looking for work in other planets, and it proved very difficult for Quist to find anyone sensible enough to find out what was wrong with the system.

The Supreme Court of Appeal on Jupiter passed some scathing remarks about the judgebot system. This court was still run by individuals, and they had become increasingly critical of the lower court's judgebots, having to reverse too many of their decisions to produce some semblance of order out of the overall sentencing system and, more to the point, giving them an additional workload.

Quist recalled that there had been a similar problem on Earth with the judgebots, but there, they'd had ample expertise to call in, and things had soon been made right. Maybe on Jupiter, he thought, the Earth's electronic connections were different from those on Jupiter where it seemed they came and went with variable intensity at different times of the season. What he did know was that these variations had certainly not been built into them as they had not shown themselves until now.

He decided that rather than lose this marvellous lucrative business, it would pay him to go and try to bring over an expert from Earth. In the meantime, when government on Jupiter was asking questions about who had installed the judgebots and what was going to be done about it, he volunteered that he could guarantee to have them fixed up in a very short time.

The judges took him at his word for the present and decided that all cases would now be heard in the Supreme Court in the interim as a temporary measure but warned him that the judgebots would be scrapped if they couldn't be fixed soon.

Amongst the politicians, they were in two minds whether they actually wanted robot judges in the system. After all, they did save a great deal of money for the inhabitants, but on the other hand, their existence kept the live judges on their toes, lest they be replaced to achieve further economy, which was always seen as good government by the populace when election times came round.

Much of what constituted parliamentary democracy and good justice, hand in hand with the rule of law, had all found their way into Jupiter's society. But as on Earth, there were gangs who were gradually expanding, wanting nothing better than an easy living without work, and who were constantly seeking out different scams to upset the order of things.

And as on Earth, further other disruptive factions had gradually evolved out of greed, and hand in hand with an increasing criminal element, the norms were breaking down. It was soon recognised generally that much had to be done, and quickly, to reverse this downward spiral.

Were there any individuals who could put things right and bring law and order, together with justice, back together into what they had begun colloquially referring to as the desired Justice Quotient? everyone wondered.

CHAPTER SEVENTEEN

· · · · · · ●●● ● ●●● · · · · ·

Quist got himself on to the first space taxi he could find and landed at Heathrow Airport in London. He had a prearranged meeting with Zooba, and as soon as Zooba saw him, he knew something wasn't right.

Quist explained how the judges in the Galaxy Court of Justice were having problems with the judgebots and also how life on Jupiter was becoming more difficult because of overpopulation caused by catastrophes on neighbouring planets. Those who survived were being encouraged by special tax allowances to have larger families to counterbalance their losses, but things had been overdone, which exacerbated the problem further.

Zooba responded by saying, 'I'm sure we can resolve the judgebot situation, but what concerns me more is what we experienced on Earth when we were almost overcome by the practices of criminals and where the judges themselves, being underpaid, were blatantly open to bribery for lenient sentences.

'So far as Jupiter is concerned, do you recall the discoveries we made in the galaxy with our first Cassini probe? We found that one of Saturn's moons, Enceladus, had all the makings of being able to tolerate the existence of Man.

'It seemed, at first, to be an unlikely place for a primitive life form, but observations showed that the ice crystals belching out through its crust contained huge carbon-based molecules which, at that time, were extremely rare in the solar system.

'When humans finally took the plunge and managed to land there, we found it capable of supporting all life forms, and since we then found a sister moon with similar attributes, I can see no problem in your kind occupying that other one when it comes to it as it remains unoccupied at present, so far as I am aware.'

Quist asked if Zooba would help and come back to Jupiter with him to sort out the judgebots and in relocating the population. At first, Zooba expressed his reluctance because he was quite well off doing what the prime minister had put him in charge of, but he said he was prepared to go and see him in case he felt it would serve a useful purpose but that he couldn't personally see what that could be.

He made an appointment for the next day at No. 10 and took Quist with him in case he needed any backup on details of life on Jupiter. Quist was dressed up to look as close to a human as possible in case anyone was frightened by his appearance or thought another invasion of aliens had started. The Press were always present outside No. 10, and it wouldn't do to set them off conjecturing about this particular arrival.

The prime minister kept her composure when she saw him as, up-close, he was quite an unusual sight. Apart from his drawn face, similar to some monkeys, she could see that he was all skin and bones, with very little flesh, obviously caused by the conditions where he came from.

They sat down together, with the prime minister's aide taking notes, and Zooba outlined the problems as he saw them.

Frances, the prime minister, said that she couldn't see any problem in finding a computer expert to go and fix the judgebots, but the social problem of gangs and the lack of living space were ones which we, ourselves, were still trying to resolve on Earth.

As Zooba knew, she said, adventurers had already been up to Enceladus to start the beginnings of an alternative for Man to live in when the time came, and as for the sister moon, she had always understood this was to be kept in reserve in case Enceladus became overpopulated or, through some major disaster, itself became uninhabitable.

Zooba said, 'It looks as though we all have the same problem, but what about the third sister moon that we've just discovered? This one too seems capable of supporting life. It is so newly discovered that it still only has the name Moon 3, but maybe we could help the aliens to relocate there so we could all eventually live in peace together, side by side.

'We'd have to make sure that Moon 3 can support alien life. So with your permission, prime minister, I can go back up to Jupiter with Quist, and between us with experts, we can organise the best solutions for everyone.'

Prime Minister Frances replied, 'I have no problem with that idea, but who will you take? I know. What about taking Basil with you from my PMG group? He has always proved excellent with our electronic problems and also has a legal background. And Stephanie can accompany you as she has a degree in population control and general social matters.

'We'll finance the expeditions, just as we are doing with the construction of the second portal in the veil around the world. Indeed, come to think of it, if we find that we can all live in peace on neighbouring planets in the future, there will be no need to have a second or any portal after all! We can spend the money more usefully that way instead.'

'What a grand scheme you have visualised, prime minister!' Zooba said.

Quist said he thought the prime minister was brilliant and that all that his fellow beings wanted was simply to live in peace with Man and not have to waste valuable resources constantly looking to Earth as their next safe haven. If it could be made to work, it would be a wonderful solution to everyone's problems.

'So let's see,' Frances said, 'who will we send up with your party? We've got you, Zooba, and you'll need an aide to cope with a lot of the details, and Quist can find his own assistant when he gets back.

'That leaves Basil and Stephanie. I'll speak to them about the details and explain things to them. They'll need some secretarial assistance to keep track of such a large venture, and any equipment they need can be decided by them before you all leave.'

Quist said that he knew just the right place—called Iso, near the airport on Jupiter—where they could establish their headquarters, and that he would send a message back to get them to prepare it.

Prime Minister Frances said that this didn't sound like a good idea because they might misunderstand and think it was all a cover for an invasion of Jupiter by Man and that it would be far better first to arrive and then gather the notables together and explain their plans. Meantime, she would notify the US President of their plans, which she felt sure he would approve of.

The settled protocol between them was to keep each other informed of major world events so that appropriate steps could be taken on each side of the Atlantic and resources appropriated accordingly, under their special relationship.

Zooba said she was quite right and wondered if she could make an office available as a control centre at the London end, and this was soon organised up the road from No. 10, in Whitehall.

The exploration party gathered together there, and it was left to Quist to raise the question of suitable garments for the humans to wear on the journey. The alien beings had already resolved the question by inventing an invisible pressure suit for themselves, and although it meant delay, he sent a message back that he wanted similar garments made up for use by humans which were to be sent as soon as they were ready. He was told it wouldn't take long; they just needed an idea of their measurements, which he organised.

The group made themselves comfortable whilst they waited and often went across to a nearby restaurant to eat and chat.

Sitting together, Basil asked Quist what it was like living on his planet, and he replied that it is very much like living on Earth. There was too much population for the resources they had, and there were endless squabbles over territory, quite often leading to fighting, with more and more sophisticated weaponry created to either defend one's territory or, as was more often the case, to frighten the others into better behaviour, everyone knowing, whilst all this went on, that if these advanced weapons were ever actually used, they could blow the whole planet to pieces or at least destroy all its inhabitants. 'It had become a very worrying place to live in,' he said.

They all returned to their base waiting for the special space garb to arrive, and to pass the time, they exchanged a few odd stories about human beings and the way they live.

Stephanie began with one about a donkey: There was a junior school in olden times in the East where the pupils were a mix of clever and stupid. The latter constantly tried the patience of the teacher, and losing his temper and it being a hot day and with the windows open, he shouted, 'You're such asses I don't know how to teach sense into you. Nevertheless, I've turned asses into men before, and I intend to do the same now'.

Only the last part was overheard by a passing stranger who was childless, and she thought how wonderful if the teacher could turn her donkey into a young man. So she waylaid him on his way home, and after her endless persistence, finally taking pity on her, the teacher said he would do it for her. He said what it would cost and that she should bring the money and donkey to him, and he would help.

He took the money when she arrived back, saying what a fine donkey it was and how it would make a great young man for her. He secretly arranged later for the donkey to be put up in a friend's farm.

The woman was ill for quite a while, and when she'd recovered and returned, the teacher asked where she had been all this time as he had turned her donkey into a man who had become famous locally, so much so that he had become the very important mayor of the district, and she'd better go and see him.

'Well, will he recognise me?' she asked.

'Certainly,' he said, 'but to make sure, take his old feeding bag with you. He'll certainly remember that.'

The woman was delighted. Her son had become a very important man, and she was going to see him!

When she arrived at the town hall, the committee was in full public session, and there, sitting at the centre of the high table, in charge, was the mayor—her famous son. She tried to catch his eye, but he didn't see her, so she moved closer and waved the feeding bag at him in front of everyone, shouting, 'It's me. Don't you know me?'

He asked her to be brought forward so he could see her more clearly, and she was delighted that this meant he now knew her after all.

'What's all this nonsense?' he asked her. And being taken aback by this rejection, she shouted back at him that he was her donkey and had been turned into the mayor, and to prove it, here was his very own feeding bag. 'So lets go home,' she said.

'Clear the room!' he shouted. 'I've had enough of this nonsense. We'll resume in half an hour.'

The woman was also sent packing with the others, so she went straight back to the teacher, calling him out of the classroom, and told him what had happened and asked him to turn that horrible man back into her donkey.

He replied that it would cost more money, but it could cost half in her case as she was so disappointed. So she should come back with the money, and to save time, he would change the mayor back into her donkey.

Off she went, and he had her own donkey brought back from the friend's stables in the meantime.

'What a naughty donkey you've been,' she shouted at her donkey when she returned. 'I suppose I wasn't good enough for you when you were mayor!'

As she went off sitting on her donkey, the teacher laughed his head off at the stupidity of this woman. How like some of his pupils, he thought!

Quist said it was a wonderful story and that they had donkeys back on Jupiter but didn't think they could ever become mayors.

'Talking of donkeys', Basil said, 'a man was on his horse going to his doctor to get some medication for his elderly wife.

'The doctor said, "I want her to take two of these pills each day but only on Saturday, Sunday, and Monday and to then skip the remaining days of the week."

'A month later, he returned to inform the doctor that his wife had sadly died of a heart attack.

'"I don't understand it," said the doctor. "She had no history of heart problems. I hope it wasn't a side effect of the medication."

'"Oh no," said the husband. "The pills were fine. It was all that skipping that killed her!"'

Quist thought he'd join in with the banter and said, 'An elderly man returned from hospital looking very worried.

'"What's the matter?" asked his wife.

'"The consultant said I have to take one of these tablets every day for the rest of my life," he replied.

'"Well, that's not too bad," said the wife, trying to cheer him up.

'"It is," said her husband. "He only gave me enough for seven days!"'

They had no time for further stories as they had a message that the special clothing was about to arrive.

On their way back to the airport, Zooba told Quist that it had only recently been revealed that Man had been trying to capture an Unidentified Flying Object, or a UFO as they had become commonly known.

'They wanted to investigate how they were capable of great speeds, sharp manoeuvres, be virtually invisible to radar, and have mastered stationary flight. This was all with the intention of copying these technologies into superfast planes, but so far, they had never managed to catch one,' he said.

Quist said that it wouldn't have made any difference if they had, and it would have been a complete waste of effort because they all had inbuilt self-destruct devices, which were triggered if the internal sensors recorded an unidentified person trying to enter. But this only took place, of course, after the occupants had been ejected safely.

Once they were all happily living in peace side by side, Quist said he would show him inside one—after switching off its protective device, of course—but he would first need special permission from Jupiter's administration to be able to do so.

......•......

The special space clothing having arrived and fitted, the party set off for Jupiter. Soon after they took off, they were confronted by several spaceships which demanded details of their journey. Being dissatisfied with their response, these ships forced them to stop by discharging several shots nearby and made them hover in-flight whilst a boarding party of aliens forced their way in. Their leader said that they would be allowed to continue their journey so long as one of their number could accompany them until they had landed.

As he said it, he suddenly spotted Quist, whom he knew to be of a very high rank in their society. He went up to him and apologised for having treated them that way but said he was only doing his duty by stopping everyone who came by. He, with others, was checking everything to ensure their own safety.

Quist said that he had heard of no such orders for interceptions to take place, but in reply, he was told that the promulgation had only just been passed whilst he was away and that this was the first interception they'd carried out.

It had appeared, he said, that Martians had started looking around the galaxy for themselves to find elsewhere to live, which is why they were carrying out more spot checks on spaceships, waylaying them in flight in the hope that the Martians knew somewhere unknown as yet to anyone else.

Before leaving, they were invited to a meal with the group, and they then left very amicably. However, as the other ships swooped away out of sight, they were stopped again by a different group of spaceships.

CHAPTER EIGHTEEN

t transpired that these craft had indeed come from Mars and were known amongst alien beings to be a much more difficult sect to cope with. Even as they entered the spaceship, they were obviously different. They all wore identical space uniforms, which gave them the appearance of being a military force. Not only that, but they spoke in an unusual guttural way, even for alien beings.

Their leader, who asked to be known as Swarof, demanded to know why alien beings were there with human beings. Quist said that they were all on their way back to Jupiter, hoping to restore law and order and to review their justice system and that he was going to introduce everyone when they got there. He asked if Swarof had any problem with that.

He replied, 'Yes, I do, in fact. We are ourselves searching the galaxy and don't seem to be able to find a better place to live instead of on Mars. How far have you got with your search?'

Now Quist wasn't going to reveal all his hands. After all, if they eventually found that Moon 3 was suitable for their own alien beings, he wasn't going to reveal everything that Man's research had discovered about the place. The last thing any of them wanted was to let the Martians move into Moon 3, and they would all then be back where they started, without any ultimate safe haven!

So he said, 'It's proving more difficult than any of us ever imagined. Our fellow citizens on Jupiter expect us to find somewhere else to be able to live if it comes to it, and we really feel that we have failed them. Indeed, when we get back, we will have to tell them that we are going to have to make do with what we have on Jupiter, which is why we have brought some humans with us to use their superior brainpower simply to make life there more satisfactory and to help us overcome the problems.

'If, by some chance, we can find an alternative place in the galaxy in the meantime, so well and good, but otherwise, it means our descendants will face certain extinction when Jupiter implodes. What luck have you had?'

Swarof replied that they were more or less at the same stage and the thought crossed his mind whether they could pool their resources, but he didn't suggest it at that stage, as his followers might not like the idea and could easily depose him for suggesting it.

After all, he thought, Martians had been brought up to believe that they were the most superior of all alien beings, and it would take a great deal for them now to believe that they needed help from anyone else.

It then occurred to him that instead of these humans going to try to fix up Jupiter before it disintegrated, why not take them with him back to Mars where they could use their brainpower for their benefit instead.

He settled on this plan, and with their greater strength, they got Basil and Stephanie, each with their assistants, into Swarof's spaceship without any trouble. Fortunately, and although no one had thought about it, the air pressure conditions were suitable there for the humans in their specially designed spacesuits. There was relief all round when this was found to be the case.

As they left, Yost quietly said to Basil that for his friend Zooba's sake, he would let the prime minister know what had happened, and no doubt, he would arrange for them to be rescued somehow. Basil told this to Stephanie, and they were both relieved to hear it, although they naturally wondered how this could be achieved.

Basil was naturally extremely concerned about being taken with his fellow humans to Mars instead of Jupiter. He set up a light-hearted conversation with Swarof, concealing his dread of being taken there.

It had long been known that Mars was a very inhospitable place for humans. Fighting between different groups was often breaking out there with innocents being caught in the crossfire, and it was the last place he wanted Stephanie to go to either as, apart from everything else, he realised he had grown a soft spot for her.

He said to Swarof, 'Has anyone told you about Man's diseases—the ones they carry with them everywhere they go? Some of them are so virulent that they have wiped out whole swathes of my countrymen, so much so that there are parts of Earth which are now uninhabitable. When you look at Earth from space, you now see large areas covered in water which would still have been land, and those living there hadn't got drowned. Is that what you want for your people? Have you noticed how I am sniffing through my nose [adding an extra one for good measure]? That's because some bacteria have got in and can well develop into influenza, one of Man's most virulent and dreaded complaints.

'We suffer from cancer, which eats away at our bodies until there is nothing left and we die, and there are so many other diseases we have, such as diabetes, which can cause our legs having to be removed because of bad circulation, or strokes where our very brains get damaged or kill us.

'Maybe, you should give serious thought to these diseases before taking us to Mars.'

The response he got was astonishing, to say the least.

Swarof calmly said that Man was far behind Martians in pharmaceutical development. 'What we did', he said, 'many decades ago was to take each newborn baby at birth and eradicate from its genes all diseases of the types outlined by Basil. We now live healthy lives right up to the time we die, so I have no intention of turning back.'

Basil put on an expression of great surprise and said, 'But don't you see, that is the very reason why your people have no immunity against our diseases. In our case, when we have measles, say, the very illness gives us protection against catching it again because our bodies grow what are called antibodies which fight off any further attack.

'Your people don't have that sort of protection, and if we stay with you much longer, I'm afraid you will drop like flies, and there will be nothing we can do to help you.'

That did it! Swarof wasn't completely crazy to want to take diseases back to Mars, never mind what he might already have contracted himself.

He said, 'Do you think it's too late for us? Have we caught something fatal from you already, Basil?'

Basil realised he'd done the trick. So he thought for a moment and said, 'Our diseases aren't catchable before twelve hours after exposure to them, so we just have enough time for you to get us back to London where we can decontaminate your spaceship just to make sure no disease is harbouring in it. And you can then go off safely.'

Naturally, this made good sense to Swarof, and he gave orders to redirect the ship to land at London as quickly as possible whilst he kept his eyes closely glued to his timepiece and a cloth over his nose and mouth.

· · · · · · · · · ● ● ● · · · · · · · · · ·

Yost had been true to his word and had notified the prime minister's office how the humans had been taken off to Mars by Swarof. The message came in during the middle of the night and was written down by a very sleepy operative—so sleepy, in fact, that the piece of paper with the message fell to the floor without it being noticed. He must have had too much to drink whilst celebrating his birthday the day before.

Next morning, it was only due to the efficiency of the cleaner that it was spotted and handed in to be logged and then handed to the prime minister.

Imagine his surprise when just as he opened and read it, in walked Basil and the others! One moment he was reading that they'd been taken off to Mars to some horrible fate, and the next minute, they'd arrived in his office! Swarof had certainly made sure to get them back quickly!

Explanations took a while to recount, at the end of which the prime minister was horrified to think that they might all have been lost to the world if it had not been for Basil's quick thinking and resourcefulness, and he commended him on it.

'It was well bearing in mind for the future that if any incursions came to Earth, they could be frightened off by the mention of these strange-sounding human diseases,' he said.

Basil said, 'That's true, but only so long as they understand our language. Otherwise, if they can't, we won't be able to frighten them into leaving, never mind communicating with them!'

'Well, we'll just have to hope for the best,' came the reply. 'We know they're advanced in many ways, so let's hope they're all taught languages, especially English, as they grow up.

'Now what about the spaceship you arrived in? What's happened to that? It would be very interesting to examine it.'

'We were very lucky with that,' came the reply. 'I'd managed to send a secret message to the airport of our impending arrival, and they had grouped together several fire engines, all hidden away. As soon as we were coming in to land, they all rushed to our ship, and standing all around it, they extended their ladders over us so there was no way Swarof could escape in it. We were trapped and led outside, leaving the spaceship available for inspection as soon as you want to arrange it.'

'Yes, but where is Swarof? What's happened to him? We don't want swarms of Martians coming to get him back.'

'We've got him locked up in an isolation cell at the airport police station. You can go and see him for yourself or send someone else. That's no problem.'

The prime minister said, 'Well, yes, there is. What if it's true that whilst it is said that they don't have diseases but instead they're mere carriers? You know, just like what happened with us? We won't have any resistance, and it could cause havoc.

'Much as we'd like to inspect a spaceship made in Mars, we'll have to be sensible and let it go, and Swarof with it. Some strange untreatable disease might be lurking in it, which we could well do without even if we use our special protective clothing.'

Bail said, 'Maybe we can do something useful before we let them go. We could send a remote-controlled vehicle inside it, which could take samples and pictures, just as we would do if we'd landed on Mars. Wouldn't that be sensible?'

'Oh, I don't know,' the prime minister replied.

'But why not?' Basil asked him. 'Don't forget, Stephanie and I have spent quite a bit of time in there and don't seem to have suffered any ill effects!'

The prime minister couldn't get himself to say the obvious, in case it frightened them. They might well have picked up some disease which hadn't yet taken hold and brought them down. But on the other hand, he couldn't simply let them free amongst the population. He finally decided that they must be put in an isolation hospital until any outcome was seen, and he told them so.

They were to be taken to the scientific research facility at Porton Down, near Salisbury in Wiltshire, England, where they would check them out and monitor for any unusual signs of disease. Once they were satisfied, they could be released and continue with the government's work, as before.

CHAPTER NINETEEN

· · · · · · ●●● ● ●●● · · · · · ·

Swarof simply couldn't believe his luck. Without any explanation, he was being released on the prime minister's orders, and his spaceship was taking him out of Earth's orbit, much to his relief.

Decontamination vehicles were then brought in to clear the site where it had stood, and the whole area was eventually declared safe for human travellers.

The Porton Down facility had been stretched to breaking point because nerve agents had again been used by foreign powers inside Britain, and each time, their operatives were required to go and find suitable samples for testing, causing many backlogs.

This caused delay, which prevented any thought of Basil and Stephanie getting back quickly to join Yost on the planned expedition to Jupiter, until they were declared properly fit.

Unfortunately for him, just as the prime minister had feared, Basil had succumbed to a very high body temperature accompanied by aching muscles and joints. The hospital was taking no chances with him and isolated him from all but one nurse who volunteered to look after him, and even she was heavily dressed in protective clothing every time she attended him.

All the monitors in his room showed very abnormal high readings for a couple of days, but after that, with some newly devised treatment which the scientists tried out on him, which had not yet been formally certificated, he made a gradual recovery and was able to be released.

As for Stephanie, she was much luckier and had been released home after just four days.

........●........

Back in Yost's spaceship, he was furious that Swarof had made off with Yost's humans whom he had planned could bring much experience to Jupiter, with a view to bringing some semblance of law and order back there.

Naturally, he wondered what had happened to them and had no idea if they'd ended up on Mars, as Swarof intended, or had they managed to escape his clutches. So imagine his surprise when he saw, flying past as if nothing untoward had happened, none other than Swarof's own distinguishable spaceship, merrily on its course back to Mars.

Yost had no idea who was in this other ship. He certainly didn't want to destroy it in case his friends were in it, so he decided on the next best thing. He pressed a special control button which made his ship become completely invisible and then made straight for Swarof's ship, which he was able to capture by taking them unaware that he was close by. And he extended the thick meshing he had devised all around it before they had a chance to stop the procedure being completed.

Swarof was shocked, to say the least. He pressed this button and that, but there was no way he could get free and, in the end, gave up the struggle and awaited his fate with some trepidation. How could this have happened after all he'd just been through? he wondered.

The next moment, in walked Yost with some of his regular crew, fully armed. He looked around for Basil and Stephanie and, being unable to see them, demanded to know where they were. When he heard the whole story, he was dumbfounded. So they must be safely back in Britain, he decided. So he didn't have to worry about them after all. There were more immediate matters to attend to.

What, for instance, was he to do about Swarof? Should he let him go back to Mars and be free to cause more trouble, or was there some way in which he could use him? And then it came to him. There must have been many developments in Martian spaceships which his scientists didn't know about.

Maybe the best plan was to take the enmeshed ship across to Jupiter where it could be examined for any useful novel installations which they could adopt for themselves, and with that superior information on top of their own, he could bring an end, at last, to the endless warring between Mars and Jupiter.

Without discussing matters with Swarof any further, he set course for Jupiter where, after advance warning, they had prepared a special hangar to receive both ships. They landed outside. The meshing mechanism was still intact so it was able to be withdrawn, and Swarof's spaceship alone was trundled inside with him in it.

Swarof himself was put into an isolation unit and kept at the airport for such eventualities, and their scientists had a field day poring over every square inch of his spaceship for any device they didn't already have and could add to their own design.

It was the first time they had got hold of the enemy's design, and so they took great care to make the most of this once-in-a-lifetime opportunity to examine it closely. It could make all the difference between failure or success in their efforts to resist the advances against their planet that had already gone on for so long, they realised.

What they found astonished them. There was gadgetry far superior to their own, especially to do with propulsion. Plans were drawn up based on these discoveries coupled with their own design, producing the very latest in speed, hovering ability, and military installations, the likes of which had been previously unheard of in Jupiter.

With all this new capability, it was realised that not only could they now successfully resist any further onslaught by the Martians but they would also now be in a position to attack them where they lived if need be. Any point in attacking rather than just resisting depended on whether there was much life left in Mars's own existence to make it worth moving in, or if they would only find it shortly afterwards disintegrating from having imploded on itself.

These were not questions for Yost to resolve. He would leave it to his government, hopefully to make the right decisions about all these major matters.

CHAPTER TWENTY

· · · · · • • ● • • • • · · · ·

Now that Yost was safely back and Swarof's spaceship had been usefully examined in great detail, his thoughts turned to Basil and Stephanie and, indeed, to his old pal Zooba.

He decided to go to Britain to report everything personally to the prime minister, and in the process, he would be able to find out for himself what had happened to the humans he knew.

Whenever a spaceship appeared in the skies over London, the protocol laid down by the prime minister required communication to be established immediately to ensure it was not a marauding attacker, and so this happened in his case.

A secret code had been specially set up to identify his particular spaceship, and so it was not long before Yost had passed through the portal and landed in Horse Guards Parade, behind No. 10, where he was admitted to that famous building and into the soundproofed room used for all secret meetings.

When the prime minister came, it was obvious that he was delighted at the fact that whilst Yost was describing all the events that had taken place, he had survived them all.

He said, 'I've got a meeting starting shortly, and I have invited your three friends, together with some technical officials whom I think will be needed. We will be holding this COBRA meeting down the road, so I can take you there with me.

'We'll be discussing how we can bring law and order back to Jupiter because I think that in the long run going forward, we humans might well need to relocate there. The natural disasters we are experiencing here, occurring with more and more severity, are giving cause for great concern, and we simply have to make preparations for a wholesale departure from Earth in the not-too-distant future.

'For example, as you may have heard, we have experienced earthquakes up to point 9 on the Richter Scale in places which have never had any there before. Buildings, even well built ones, have collapsed. Previously thought extinct volcanoes have suddenly come to life, spewing out molten lava and destroying whole populations. The gases they've produced have polluted the atmosphere, so much so that our planes and spaceships have been grounded for weeks at a time for safety reasons.

'We've had torrential rain falling even on our deserts and drought where populations normally live. Fires have ravaged our forests and ruined our houses because our world now suffers from unusually extended periods of drought. So all in all, we are fighting a constant battle on Earth against these natural forces. How long this can go on is anyone's guess, but clearly there is no time to lose in finding where else we can live safely in the future.'

They made their way to the COBRA meeting room, and Yost was delighted to see his old human friends once again there. He went up to them and said how pleased he was to see them, and they said how glad they were that he had survived so many dangerous experiences.

The prime minister opened the meeting in his customary way, welcoming his guests and introducing them to the regular members of the committee and especially the new ones. He then went on, 'I wish to discuss a most urgent and important matter with you all. It is to do with the future of our population. You have all seen how nature is gradually taking control of our environment with daily reports of disasters and constant states of emergency having to be declared, followed by more and more demands on our resources. Whole streets of houses have been washed away by exceptional torrential rain and many people left homeless. Our winters have been intolerable, with lengthy freezing cold spells and stifling hot summers, as you know.

'This may be all due to a natural breakdown in the Earth's environment or too much CO_2 still being discharged by us into the atmosphere, leading to what has become known as global warming, despite all the treaties countries have signed up to in order to reverse the process. We have certainly been warned by our scientists that the oceans are rising and our coastal towns are likely to be inundated as a consequence, with loss of life where rescue has become impossible.

'Just consider the enormous iceberg that floated perilously near a village in north-west Iceland with large pieces falling off into the sea as it went by, causing mini tsunamis and the waves constantly threatening to suddenly swamp the village without warning.

'Looking around the galaxy as our scientists have been doing, we have come to the conclusion, by a large majority, that Jupiter is our best bet for relocation when we are finally forced to leave. It is not so urgent that it has to take place straight away, but certain basic but important preparations have to be made well in advance, as you would expect of a responsible government, especially having to deal with an unknown planet.

'It will be a major undertaking to convince the population that they should leave and give up their homes and all their possessions as they can only be allowed a few small items each on the journey. Once the plan is put into effect, the population will find that their properties have become valueless overnight as nobody will want to buy them since nearly everyone will be leaving. And there will be no demand for them any more. Any thought of compensation has to be ruled out, being such a major undertaking.

'Of course, there will be some, such as those who, through old age or infirmity, are unable to undertake space travel and will have to be left behind. So we will make a special payment to such of their chosen relatives who opt to stay behind with them until they die, after which they can then follow the others there. We will also provide social housing for those relatives who eventually follow on until they can get on their own feet in the new community on Jupiter.

'Apart from all that, I want you to realise that Jupiter has become somewhat lawless for the usual reasons of greed and an unwillingness to earn a living on the part of certain gangs and the underworld, and so before we can think of actually going there to live, we must ensure that law and order is restored. Otherwise, we could be virtually no better off by going to all the trouble of going there and then losing our lives.

'This is why I have devised a plan to deal with this problem. We need to replicate what we achieved on Earth when we sent delegates out amongst different peoples and cultures resulting in law and order, together with justice being steadily restored to the citizens.'

'I remember what happened,' Zooba said, butting in. 'The delegates, mostly lawyers, went out with a new system of court procedures and were met with a variety of resistant ploys which, in many cases, made them scurry back with their tails between their legs, lucky that they had got back in one piece.'

'That's right. Remind me of the new court procedures though,' the prime minister asked.

Zooba replied, 'Well, instead of the final appeal court remaining within each jurisdiction, it was made known that final judgements or appeals would all have to be countersigned by a Supreme Court in the USA or the UK, whichever was appropriate. At a stroke, all corrupt judges were put out of business because there was no longer any point in bribing them for a favourable outcome since they no longer had the last word on their cases.

'The new procedure delayed final outcomes, of course, but justice was served properly at last, and everyone knew it.

'There was also an interim system, which worked quite well where the so-called Visiting Judges were sent out to sit in the court with the local judges and were soon able to spot signs of corruption, such as a lenient sentence like community service being imposed in a serious case, which really warranted incarceration in prison. In such cases, the Visiting Judge was able to halt the release of the accused, refer the final decision abroad as before, and the corrupt judges promptly sacked and charged with corruption in high office.'

The prime minister said, 'Well, that's exactly what we'll do on Jupiter. Now what I want to know, Yost, is how many different countries exist at present in Jupiter, what sort of infrastructure and communication exists there, what the terrain is actually like there, and what human-type food is available. Do you have shops, for example?

'I'm sure there's so much you can tell us which will make our colonisation run smoothly. You've seen what we have here on Earth, so how do the two compare?'

Yost was a little taken aback by this onslaught of questions and asked if the prime minister wouldn't mind if he could have a few words with his friend Zooba before proceeding. His request was granted, and the meeting adjourned for half an hour.

The two went into a corner, and Zooba said, 'I know what is troubling you, Yost. You feel that you might be betraying your fellow beings if you give all this information to the prime minister, but you must realise that he only needs it so as to be able to plan the colonisation peacefully for your people.'

'It's not that,' Yost said. 'I just don't know all the answers! The prime minister will think I'm not cooperating and will be upset with me. I'd like to answer his questions, but you see, I've lived quite a solitary life there.'

'Well, I'll explain it to him for you, and you just do your best to answer,' came the reply.

Zooba went over to the prime minister and explained things and said Yost will do his best with his questions.

Yost started by saying, 'I'm honoured to be part of your important group, Prime Minister, and wish to be as helpful as possible. The fact is that we only have six habitable towns in Jupiter. There are so many watery swamp areas that there's no room for more. I've heard of plans to drain areas to grow crops in, but so far as I know, nothing much appears to have been done about it because of lack of resources. As to what food humans can stomach there, I've really no idea. That will be a matter of finding out, but unless you can find out before you go, you may find it impossible to survive there.

'Maybe I could arrange for some samples of our crops to be brought for you to try. Otherwise, I can't see how you will get to know. Even then, there is the question whether Jupiter has enough food for the whole of Earth's population, assuming of course that there are enough places for them to live in as well.

'It seems to me that the only way all these requirements can be checked out is if some of your scientists were to go there and see for themselves what we actually have and what needs to be done before a mass exodus can take place.'

'Well, that is most helpful,' the prime minister responded. 'Are you willing to lead a party of humans back to Jupiter to help them see what needs to be done?'

'I would be honoured,' Yost replied, 'but first, we have to deal with the Martians who, at present, stand in our way from getting back. If you can help with constructing some spaceships, I can give them their invisibility quality, and we can steal up on the Martian spaceships and destroy them.'

'That sounds a little harsh,' the prime minister said. 'Can't we just distract them while we slip past them unnoticed? Maybe we can combine the two ideas and, using invisible spacecraft, attack just one or two to frighten them and make the rest flee from this invisible malevolent force you have in mind. That way, we can get through.'

Basil joined in the conversation at that point and said, 'Maybe I'm missing something, but surely, if we have invisible craft, we have no need to worry about the Martians. They won't even know we're passing them by!'

'Yes, that's true,' Yost responded, 'but they may pick us up on their radar and take pot shots at where it shows we are. Anyway, it's worth trying, if that's what's decided.'

'I don't know,' the prime minister said. 'It sounds to me that we would be putting our lives in danger if we took that chance. They could well destroy our craft even if they are invisible, so I think we have no choice but to destroy them and make sure.'

Yost said, 'Before I left, I remember that our researchers announced that they were working on a special ray, which was capable of being operated from a distance, some sort of special radio frequency they said. If they've perfected it and we can get hold of it, we can destroy all the Martian spaceships from a distance and not suffer at all ourselves!'

'I'll send a message back to find out, and if it is available, I can go back on my own to get it and install it in my own invisible craft. On my way back, I can destroy them, solving two problems at the same time—getting our group into Jupiter safely, and destroying our enemy, the Martians.'

'We couldn't let you risk your life like that,' the prime minister said. 'But otherwise, I really don't know the answer. Are you sure you'd be all right doing it your way?'

Yost replied bravely, 'I can see no alternative. The only way to save humanity is to help them to get out of Earth into Jupiter, and if that's the only way to achieve it, then I am prepared to risk my life for the cause. As you know, I'm particularly fond of Zooba, and if for no other reason, I would gladly risk my life for him.'

CHAPTER TWENTY-ONE

· · · · · ●●●● ● ●●●● · · · · ·

Preparations were put in place in London and Washington for the journey to Jupiter. Subcommittees were established at each end to take care of individual aspects of the task, and the prime minister put Yost in charge of matters relating to the journey and the arrival at the other end.

Before he left, he called together his own group of alien beings, with their own spaceships, to assist him on his journey to Jupiter to get hold of the special ray equipment and explained the purpose of their mission to them. Some were surprised to hear that they intended, and were able, to finally destroy the Martian enemy, and others were intrigued to hear about this new ray equipment that was going to play such a big part in the forthcoming invisible battle.

Yost chose a few whom he knew he could rely on and instructed the others to stand by ready to assist if he had to call on them if things turned ugly during the battle.

They set off at speed back to Jupiter, dodging the Martian ships with their invisible stealth equipment, and landed safely quite soon afterwards. The journey there had become shorter in recent times because Jupiter's orbit had got closer to Earth than it had been for a long time.

Some so-called experts even thought that the two might collide at some point in the future, but others were more optimistic and thought that it was just a temporary aberration. Nothing could be done about it either way, though naturally, the scientific papers were full of it, being the latest subject of conversation amongst the experts.

The group was expected at the skyport just outside the main town where everything was ready to install the new ray equipment, which the authorities had provided out of their meagre defence budget.

The equipment was installed, and they set off towards Earth to do battle with the Martians on the way.

It so happened that the Martian force was itself on its way to take over Earth by force at the same time as Yost's group was returning here, and they were intercepted with this new ray.

They didn't know which way to turn. Every time they took avoiding action, some of them disappeared, destroyed by the ray until, at last, Yost decided that they had all been defeated.

The various crews in Yost's group were delighted. At last, their worst enemy, the Martians, had been defeated! Or so they thought.

One of the Martian ships had got away without it being noticed and then, having seen what had happened to the others, came back and made a desperate attempt to attack one of Yost's group, only to be destroyed by the ray before it could get near enough to it.

Arriving back on Earth and reporting his success against the Martians to the prime minister, Yost was commended profusely. At last, they could now adopt the next part of their plan and go to Jupiter safely to find out the answers to all the questions they needed answering.

In conjunction with the PMG group and its special advisers, the party was assembled at a secret skyport just outside London, and with Yost as the leading captain, they took off for Jupiter.

Looking out as they approached, they saw that the terrain was vast but desolate. Large parts of the surface were covered in some sort of liquid, maybe water, which reflected the light, but they couldn't be sure until they got closer. On what parts they could see clearly, there were very few buildings.

In fact, they were not so much buildings as simple forms of habitation which didn't look very weather-proof to say the least. It could be, they thought, that the weather was not extreme so that what they had constructed was sufficient. Closer inspection and experience of the weather would answer both of those questions.

Yost's colleagues were waiting for their arrival, and Basil and Stephanie with the other two humans who were experts in space exploration were introduced. And they all went off into the town where they settled into a hotel-type building which had recently been constructed and which had the latest gadgets that the alien beings had invented.

Many of these items turned out to be very similar to those found on Earth. They had invented plumbing and had long ago discovered electricity, so the group felt comparatively relaxed in surroundings which seemed familiar, much to their surprise.

Basil and Stephanie stayed together in one room, and of course, some of the group had their own homes and went there to stay.

Surprisingly enough, room service was available, so Basil thought that this would be a good opportunity to find out what food existed there, so he called down for a menu. It turned out that the inhabitants didn't have formal mealtimes as those kept to on Earth, and so the menu was an all-day one and showed him everything they had for visitors.

He was astonished. It read like one you would find in any restaurant on Earth. But how could this be? He was so intrigued that he contacted Yost and asked him how they had done this.

The answer was simple, replied Yost. On one of his trips to Earth, he'd picked up one of its menus, and their chefs, having nearly all the ingredients, were able to replicate the dishes humans liked. It was done as a courtesy to human visitors, and he said he was surprised that Basil hadn't known about it. Indeed, he said, they were working on the missing ingredients in their laboratories as their citizens quite liked the change from their regular diet.

He went on to tell Basil that they had growing areas undercover where these ingredients were produced. They were specially hidden by their invisibility device in case the Martians attacked, but now that, hopefully, they had all been destroyed, there was no longer any need for such subterfuge. It had been one of the Martians' ploys to destroy food production when attacking a planet so as to bring the inhabitants to their knees and surrender, he said.

Basil was amazed to hear all this. No one, until now, had any idea what human-type food was available on Jupiter, so that answered their first main question, and he sent a message back to Earth to put the prime minister's worries at rest on that score.

The couple was accompanied by Yost around the place, and points of interest were shown. During their discussion, Basil asked Yost why there hadn't apparently been any land reclamation as it would have made it possible to extend their building and growing areas. Yost replied that it was a simple matter of resources. But if humans were to come to live there, he said, they could construct suitable dykes he'd heard about, though it would be an expensive exercise removing large tracts of water for building purposes.

Whilst the three were walking along, gunfire was heard from several places around them, and Yost said it must be some of the gangs fighting over territory. Basil thought this a good time to ask about their justice system and if law and order reigned or whether there was a lot of such gang fighting. Yost said that, unfortunately, it was becoming an increasing problem.

The authorities, especially their police, had been doing their best to clamp down on the criminals, but whenever they were brought to trial, they seemed to be back on the streets after having been given yet 'another chance' by the judiciary. This was no way to deter criminals, Basil said. There had to be bribery going on. Weren't the judges paid enough to stop them taking bribes? he asked.

'Well, that's not for me to sort out,' Yost said. 'I suspect that is the case, but I'll take you to our chief leader who knows all about these things. He's much cleverer than I am. We'll have to make an appointment, but I'm sure he'll fit us in as soon as he can.

'He is called Excellency Robert and is sure to want to meet you both. He holds town meetings in our great hall, so let's go along there and ask for an appointment.'

The great hall turned out to be a run-down construction which had seen better days. Its roof was leaking, and some windows were broken—all due, no doubt, to a shortage of resources. Basil wondered why this was so. Could it be that they had spent so much on armaments to enable them to resist invasion by the Martians that their economy had suffered so much? He thought he might broach the subject with the Excellency when he saw him, if he thought it appropriate to do so on a first meeting with him, of course.

When the message got through that they had come from Earth and wanted an audience with him, he was quick to change his diary and arranged to see them that evening. They were to go to his residence to share a meal with him and his wife.

When the three of them arrived, they were shown inside to await his presence. The whole place was decorated like a palace with ornate fittings fit for a king, entirely opposite to the humble dwellings or the meeting hall they had seen so far. Were all these the signs of profligacy, indicative of more corruption? they wondered.

Yost himself wasn't surprised because he'd grown up to know that the Excellency was always surrounded in luxury, and he'd never queried how this had come about. He'd seen him parade through the streets in his ornate carriage and horses many times whilst he grew older and, in a way, had come to expect that his home would be equally superb.

The chief leader, His Excellency, entered the room with an enormous entourage, and after everyone stood up, the three introduced themselves to him. He was dressed in sumptuous garments and went over and sat on what looked like a copy of a throne.

The first impression they had, especially the two humans, was that here, yet again, was a leader who had feathered his nest at the expense of his subjects. They could be wrong, but they would wait and see what transpired to give them a clue.

Basil then waited until he was spoken to, and Yost was the first to speak. He said, 'Your honour, I would like you to meet my very good friends Basil and Stephanie who have just arrived from Earth. We have come to see if we can assist your country with its judicial system.' They knew, from their experience on Earth, that judges are tempted to accept bribes if they are not paid enough in terms of both salaries and pensions, and it could well be that under the new system (as has been found to be the case on Earth), any corrupt judge would soon be found out if they were to install Visiting Judges to oversee their proceedings.

Another benefit of this new system was that if a judge refused to have a Visiting Judge, it would be likely that he had already been corrupted, and they could insist that it should happen or remove him.

Little did Basil know that His Excellency himself was not averse to a bit of bribery and often imposed himself on certain trials, where the judges would tip him off about a particular prisoner. He would send an emissary to the cell to inform the prisoner that he could guarantee a lighter sentence in return for a contribution to His Excellency's favourite charity—himself!

This situation, of course, made things much more difficult to resolve, but as it went on behind the scenes without Basil's knowledge, he was clearly not going to be able to make much progress with his fresh ideas for reforming the legal system.

But His Excellency was cunning and decided there could still be room for reforms and yet continue to retain his finger in the legal pie. He called the judges together and told them that instead of the previous arrangements, they were to impose unusually heavy fines on criminals as well as pass prison sentences on them and that he expected the restitution orders and fines to be channelled through to him as a form of additional tax to spend on 'good causes' for the country.

He would decide how the money was to be spent, and the net result would be that the criminal fraternity would soon find that the heavy fines and repayments were a deterrent against further criminal activity.

Naturally, the criminal gangs thought this was a step too far and had upset the previously acceptable balance between themselves and the authorities, so they decided to hold a meeting to discuss the best way to deal with the problem which His Highness had just created.

One of their members proposed that they should kidnap him and demand all the fines to be returned from his coffers, whereby he would be freed. Others weren't so sure about this idea because as soon as His Highness went missing, there would be such a hue and cry that he would be certain to be found, and them with him!

A general consensus was finally agreed upon. One of their members was to gain access to his bedroom in the night, find out, with threats of violence, where he kept his money and valuables, and then disappear with them without trace and distribute them back to the criminals. It would require immaculate timing for this cat burglar type to find his way in and get away safely afterwards, but with careful preparation, they thought that this could all be achieved successfully.

They had a particular member in mind for the task. He had once carried out a similar raid for them on a criminal's home because the others thought he'd been cheating them over a particular scam, and whilst that entry had been successful, they realised that it was going to be much more difficult in His Highness's case because it was to be expected that he would be constantly surrounded by day and night guards.

They managed to inspect the original plans of His Highness's new residence, which was most helpful, by gaining access to the office of the architect who had designed it. His name was still visible on the board outside the construction site's office, which had not yet been removed because the grounds of the residence were still being finished off.

The plans showed them where the master bedroom was where His Excellency slept, so the being managed to slither in through an extractor ducting and soon found himself outside the bedroom but then spotted a guard on duty. He decided to get back into the ducting and wait until the guard went off for something.

It was a long wait and was getting light, but eventually, the guard left his post, and the man peeped inside the bedroom, only to see that it was occupied by a member of staff and not His Excellency at all! They had obviously switched rooms for security purposes.

So where was His Excellency sleeping then? It was impossible to know, which was just what the security officers had intended. But his luck was in. He spotted a servant carrying a tray along the corridor, and it could only be meant for his master, so he followed, being careful not to be seen by hiding behind a pillar. As soon as the servant knocked on a particular door, asking, "May I come in, your Excellency?" he knew that this was the right room.

He bided his time until the servant had gone, and as there was no guard at that moment for some reason, he burst into the room, flourishing a gun, shouting that he wanted the money from the fines that had been collected from the criminals.

In response, The Highness, without hesitation, pulled out a gun from under the sheets and shot him dead on the spot!

He had been prepared for such an attack for some time and knew exactly what to do when it finally occurred. His wife screamed in horror, and two guards who'd returned came rushing in to see what was wrong, only to find the body on the floor.

The guards were put under arrest for having left the room unguarded, putting His Excellency's life in jeopardy, and they were tried for treason and hanged.

· · · · · · · · · · ● · · · · · · · · · ·

Time passed, and the criminals called another meeting to decide what to do in face of the miserable failure of the previous attempt. But as soon as they had decided to carry out an assassination whilst His Excellency was in his vehicle, going from one event to another, he suddenly dropped dead in his sleep, to everyone's amazement!

There was no way they could now get their excessive fines back, or was there? Presumably, they thought, everything that he owned would be passed on to his wife, but what if the new Excellency, once appointed, insisted that in return for her life, she should hand it all over to him? Nothing was impossible in those dangerous times, so if they were going to have any redress, they had better act quickly.

She had felt very insecure once her husband had died and had gone to stay with her mother until the new elections were over. The criminals followed her there and demanded the money, only to be told that it was in the hands of his executors, pending winding up his estate, and that there was nothing available until that had been done. They searched the place but found nothing of any value, and they left.

She and her parents had been extremely frightened by these demands and reported it all to the police. However, nothing was done about it because she couldn't identify the criminals, not that the police would have done much about it anyway, as they were almost all in the pay of the criminals. They were just told to wait to see the terms of his will, and not knowing the identity of the executors, they had no other choice but to do so.

CHAPTER TWENTY-TWO

· · · · · · ●●● ● ●●●● · · · · ·

A sudden explosion took place near where Basil and Stephanie were staying, and it turned out to be a volcano from the mountain which overlooked the place. It had wrongly been declared dormant by the local professor whose duty it was to carry out regular inspections, but he'd obviously misjudged it.

Molten lava poured down and along the streets and into the rivers, causing havoc amongst the weak wooden houses that lay in its path, a number of them soon burning and collapsing from its fierce heat. Vehicles were left overturned and piled one upon the other, making any rescue attempts futile, with the consequent loss of life being enormous.

Basil and Stephanie moved up to higher ground as soon as the first rumblings were felt, as they had experienced such an event before. They did all they could to help in the rescue effort. It was quite pitiful with very young children wandering about, crying for their parents. They were gathered up as best they could and took them to an emergency centre where some were quickly reunited, but others sadly not.

Until the election of the new Excellency had taken place, nothing more could be done except to do everything possible to bring things back to normality. When he was finally elected by a majority of the populace, it was realised that he was not self-interested like his predecessor but was seen to be the benevolent leader they'd all yearned for for such a long time.

He held his first public meeting in the main town hall, and everyone wanted to get in to see what he was going to say. They crammed themselves in, falling over in one or two cases.

The guards locked the doors once everyone was in their place, and when he stepped on to the stage, he was greeted with a standing ovation, which lasted for many minutes.

Once the crowd quietened down, he spoke to them, 'My name is Hector. I am not to be referred to as His Excellency any more, as I am a man of the people, and Leader will be my title. I've been elected as your leader after my predecessor unfortunately suddenly passed away, and I promise to rule our country with a fair hand, with everyone having a fair chance of a decent living.

'There will be no more criminals because we now have present with us the benefit of a couple of very pleasant and knowledgeable humans who are staying here to assist us. They have brought with them some novel legal plans which will put justice to the forefront of everything we do. Law and order are going to prevail as they once used to do, and everyone will benefit.

'There will be no more corruption either whilst I am in charge, and we are going to start on a novel programme of infrastructure, reclaiming our swampy land so that it can be put to proper use at last. We are told, from investigations already carried out, that some valuable minerals will be found during the reclamation, and we can sell these to other planets to pay for the work, so I don't plan to increase your taxes.'

There was a spontaneous roar of approval, with everyone present saying what a far-sighted and fair leader they now had, especially as he promised not to raise their taxes!

He went on, 'We will build on the new land and extend our territories, and there will be homes for everyone. No longer will we have to worry about the volcano exploding in our faces as we will be able to live far away from it at last. Our mass is two and a half times the size of all other planets put together, so we have ample opportunity to expand our usable lands.'

There were cheers at this point because many lives had already been lost when molten lava had suddenly enveloped their wooden shacks and destroyed them.

A roar of approval rang out from his subjects, and Hector knew that he now had them all in his grasp and had won them over despite a few dissenting voices, which were soon silenced.

He touched on other matters, such as medical care for those who had accidents, and then closed the meeting to more rousing applause but without taking any questions as it had been so stipulated in advance. He wasn't prepared to be taken by surprise by some clever reporter with awkward questions before he had even got his feet under the table.

Back in his private rooms, Hector asked to see Basil and Stephanie. He was keen to get the reforms under way as quickly as possible and told them that they should tell him that whatever additional expertise was needed from Earth that they thought necessary, it would be arranged for them.

Basil said that in the first place, he certainly wanted Yost to help them and told Hector what an enormous help he had been so far with the wonderful protective ring around Earth which he had organised.

Hector replied that it might be useful for Jupiter to have one as well, but he would give it further thought because of the expense involved given its size. But once they were able to top up their coffers, it could then be afforded, and they would go ahead with it.

The discussion turned to their legal system and how it was impregnated with corruption from top to bottom. Basil said that he was not surprised as this was how humans had ended up with their own legal system. Justice no longer existed until the reforms had been brought in, he said, and at Hector's insistence, he expounded on those reforms.

What they needed, he said, were some form of modernised judgeships, some sort of robots, he said. They could be loaded up with all the court precedents to be followed as that was how things were done in court and also have all their statutes downloaded into them. They could then retire all the judges since legal decisions could now be made by the judgebots in the knowledge that nothing had been missed out, and precedents followed in the usual way. It could be called automatic justice.

Hector was no fool. He said that this idea was only as good as the operatives whose task was to keep them up-to-date. 'What if a decision was passed one day, only for people to find that an unreported precedent had been created the day before which went the other way and hadn't yet been loaded up inside the robot judges because of laziness or carelessness?' he asked.

Basil answered that it must be the same problem for actual judges. Unless they were kept up-to-date, their judgements could well be flawed, and there would be endless appeals from their decisions anyway.

With Quist now out of the way, Yost was able to make progress with future plans for Jupiter's double protective canopy. However, the new leader decided one day not to spend more money on it in the hope that a new dawn of peace and prosperity would come upon them all at last, and it would prove unnecessary.

He hoped that by sharing out the available viable planets amongst the different groups, they could all live out their lives without further confrontation.

But he hadn't counted on the remaining Martians who were still keen on finding the ones who had gone missing and who were determined to continue their search for them, whatever the cost.

Their leader had decided that it should not be seen that the missing ones had been left to their fate without some show of trying to rescue them, and he formed a force of his most reliable warriors for the task.

Strangely enough, they arrived in force on Jupiter just as another group from Earth arrived, bringing some of the items Yost said he'd needed. Although they could see each other arriving, neither side was prepared for an immediate confrontation, particularly as the Martians had been ordered not to be belligerent straight away since there was no point in suffering further loss of life if their missing countrymen could be found without doing so.

They set up camp just outside the main town and made enquiries of the locals whether they had seen any of their kind, but as soon as they appeared before them and were told that they hadn't seen any of them, the locals knew that others could arrive from Mars, and war could break out at any moment. So at the first opportunity, they secretly reported that Martians had arrived and revealed where their camp was.

As for the group who'd arrived from Earth, they were put up in town, and they took the equipment they'd brought along to Yost's warehouse.

Hector was soon advised of the arrival of the Martians. This was the last thing he wanted on his plate at the beginning of his leadership, so he called a secret meeting of his closest advisers to deliberate over the situation.

It was recalled that Yost's ray had destroyed all the Martian spaceships that they had found, but it was possible that just like the one that had escaped and was eventually destroyed, it was indeed conceivable that others had landed without their knowledge, as they seemed to appear so secretly.

They sent out countrywide messages enquiring if any had been seen, and one remote village managed to get a message back that they had been overrun by a group of Martians who were holding them hostage.

Hector recalled his advisers once he'd heard about this report, and they decided to send a force to relieve the village, after which they would deal with the new arrivals.

Yost was sent along with the General in charge so that he could experience what they were like so that this information could possibly be of use in the inevitable final confrontation.

The villagers had reported that there were about twenty Martians there, and so the force sent to deal with them was of a slightly larger size. When they arrived, they found that the whole place was in lockdown. The streets were deserted, and no one was allowed out during the night-time curfew.

To deal with the situation, the General first had to locate the base where the Martians were gathered, so he sent out two of his best men to see what could be done about it. They only dared move about during daytime because of the curfew, which made matters more difficult than they might otherwise have been.

They struck upon a clever idea. They knew of a theatrical costume shop they'd spotted and went in to see if they had any Martian outfits which might have been used for one of their local plays. They had no modern entertainment in that village any more because its communication systems had long ago been destroyed by an enormous lava flow, which is why their local theatre had been restored and was so much prized.

It turned out that they'd recently put on a play involving their Martian enemies long before they'd actually arrived, and ever since then, once they had arrived, they hadn't dared use their costumes in case they got to hear of it. The Martians were always built into their plays in one way or another as they were their worst enemy, and the people enjoyed watching them made fun of.

Fortunately, the outfits were perfect fits, and the shopkeeper was happy to let them use them if it was going to help them get rid of the Martians.

It remained to be seen if the outfits were convincing, so they chanced their arm and marched down the street with an air of superiority, passing other Martians on the way. They were astonished when the others saluted them as they went by, and they realised from this that not only were the outfits convincing replicas but that they were also made to represent those worn by senior officers, which is why they were saluted.

Now at last, the two felt free to move about. As they were passing their base, they went in and shouted out who they really were to make sure they knew who they were before they had the chance to shoot them. The others thought how resourceful they'd been in getting hold of these outfits and wished them luck as they left.

Fortunately, they were able to speak the same language as the Martians, albeit with a slight accent, so they arrived at their camp and went in. The guard at the door jumped to attention and saluted them, so when they went in, they felt very confident in what they were about to do.

They asked who was in charge, and he came over to introduce himself and saluted. They told him that a group of Martians had come to collect them and that they were from that group. And now that they had found them, if they would follow them, they would take them to the others, and they could all go back to Mars together.

The one in charge had a feeling that something was wrong with all this. He couldn't put his finger on it but decided to be cautious. Something just didn't seem right.

In any case, they'd all started getting used to being in charge of the locals and could see themselves settling there instead of returning. They'd begun settling in to their houses and taking over their shops and were missing Mars less and less.

On the whole, Jupiter seemed to be a good substitute for Mars as it seemed to have everything they needed, and in fact, they were proposing to bring more Martians to set up extra colonies there.

He asked to see their identity papers, and as they had stupidly overlooked the need for any, the cat was out of the bag. They were locked up until they could be interrogated thoroughly to find out who they really were.

One of them managed to send a prearranged signal back to camp where the General had been waiting anxiously for news, and as he could now trace them from the coordinates in the message, he decided that an all-out battle couldn't be avoided if the invaders were to be resisted once and for all.

The Martian leader had been trained to be always on his guard so that when he cross-examined the prisoners as to how many more there were, he automatically assumed that he was being told lies and that although the answer he got was that there were only just a few, he assumed that they were a much larger force. This didn't worry him too much as he believed that their fighting devices were much more sophisticated than the others' were.

The General rallied his group, and they arrived during the curfew. They had to silence two of the night guards with their knives and then went in whilst they were all asleep. Some of the party went to individual houses and brought them to the place, and it wasn't long before they'd all been taken prisoner and their own two released. They were all taken back to the General's camp awaiting the next day for instructions.

If they'd intended to kill them, they could have done it where they were, but the General gave instructions not to do so unless it became essential because the plan was to send them back to Mars with some message that would convince them back there that Jupiter had too hostile an environment for Martians to live there.

The scientific laboratory in the main town had been gathering a group of viruses not just as an experiment but in case chemical warfare became essential for the planet's defence. They'd gathered these from some unfortunate humans who had been in a probe which had recently crashed on Jupiter and had then reproduced them in quantities sufficient to use in a battle. They were also working on experiments with nerve agents and their antidotes but hadn't made much progress with them yet.

The General decided that he would impregnate a couple of the prisoners with the human viruses and then send the whole lot of them back to Mars. They would soon find that the viruses killed off their victims as their bodies would have no defence against them or any treatment, and they would conclude that Jupiter was an unsafe place to be. If that wouldn't stop them coming, he thought, he didn't know what would.

It so happened that Martians were far more advanced scientifically than those in Jupiter. Their offspring were required to study science from a very early age, and it wasn't surprising therefore that when they grew up, some of them had invented previously unknown substances derived especially from certain plants only to be found on Mars.

One of these was a nerve agent, a drop of which was capable of destroying a person's body in a matter of hours. The Martian army had phials of these issued to them when they were sent on dangerous missions as an additional weapon in time of need. They had to be looked after most carefully in case the carrier killed himself with it, but it was provided with a secure closure which was designed to keep it safely inside.

And so it was that when the General's force arrived and used the deterrent of the viruses on the prisoners, they, in turn, had time to release their nerve agent on them. Absolute mayhem broke out amongst all of them as they realised that they were all doomed. Could they get medical help from anywhere in time before they succumbed to a horrible death, or was it impossible? they asked themselves.

They all decided to combine forces and make haste back to the laboratories in Mars where, hopefully, with their advanced knowledge there, they might be able to save them from a painful and certain death.

This was chemical warfare of the worst kind, but strangely, in this case, because of the nature of the weapons used, both sides had joined together to find help for their misfortune.

Arriving on Mars, they were whisked off to an experimental facility where tests showed what agent and virus had been used, and treatment was given accordingly. Some survived, only to lead lives as invalids, and others didn't make it at all, as was to be expected.

CHAPTER TWENTY-THREE

ector's advisers told him that the loss of some of his subjects this way would not do him any good and that he ought to send a force to Mars to try to bring back any of their subjects they could find. Even if only one could be brought back, he would be applauded for looking after his people.

He had his doubts about this advice. Whilst it was a terrible thing for so many to have been lost, it would certainly be worse if any more lost their lives on a rescue mission. And then there was the cost to be taken into account.

Meanwhile, Basil and Stephanie were not at all happy about this state of affairs. If Jupiter continued to remain susceptible to attack from Martians searching for an alternative home, they would be unable to concentrate on their main task of reducing crime and establishing their incorruptible judgebots in the courts.

Basil said that he hoped that the virus and nerve agents that were now in Mars would keep them at bay, but Stephanie wondered, what if they came back with the nerve agent and attacked them with it? They would be much worse off than ever. It was a pity that it had been unleashed in the first place, and what an error of judgement, she thought!

They told the Leader of their fears over this and suggested that every effort should be made to find an antidote to the nerve agent. There was no worry about the viruses because they had come from Earth, where treatments were readily available, but unknown nerve agents were a completely different matter. So he gave instructions to their laboratories to research for an antidote with all haste and provided special funds and a competition to assist them.

Basil was asked to get on with the law-and-order problem. He told the Leader that he planned to call the judges together and explain the plans to retire them on specially good pensions and not to appoint any new ones, and he obtained his permission to make them this offer.

The amount of these exceptional pensions were agreed upon quite quickly because once the judges had been retired, economic excuses would soon be found to reduce their value gradually against the cost of living anyway, the Leader told him in confidence.

Basil was an upright person, and he thought that he was not prepared to take part in such sharp practice. He didn't want to say anything at that stage but decided to bide his time. He didn't even tell Stephanie about it.

He sent an invitation to the judges to meet himself and Stephanie after close of business in the law courts. They were all naturally very keen to find out what he had to tell them, and so they all turned up without exception. He took his place at the top table, and after introducing himself and Stephanie to the judges, Basil began by saying, 'Although we have been here for some time, we have been unable to get on with the main purpose of our visit, which is to restore law and order to your country. We've experienced so many events since arriving, but now that things seem to have settled down, we feel that we can get on with matters at last.

'It is high time that justice was restored, and we have brought a plan which has been found to be very workable on Earth, and we cannot see why the same should not be achieved here.

'I realise that it is not in your remit to deal with such political matters or changes to the way things are done yourselves, so now that, hopefully, the Martians have been taught a lesson, we can get on with the reforms without any further interference from that quarter.

'Let me explain. As the main change to the existing arrangements, I have been authorised to offer you all an early retirement on very generous pensions to take effect at the end of this legal term. You will be replaced by judgebots, meaning judge robots, and in the interim, you will, of course, help us to install them in the courts or, at least, not to stand in their way.

'This will be the way forward, and there will be no more bribery in return for short sentences, not that I am suggesting, for one moment, that any of you are involved in such practices.'

The judges looked sheepishly at each other, realising that they had been tumbled, although they tried to hide it.

Then a very odd thing happened. One of the judges jumped up and shouted out that he is a Martian in the disguise of a judge and then threatened everyone there, flourishing a phial of nerve agent in the air.

He herded them all into a corner of the room whilst another so-called judge jumped up and declared that they were both there in disguise and were very surprised that they hadn't been discovered whilst appearing as judges.

But what did they want? everyone asked each other. What could these two expect to achieve on their own, they wondered, and how had they stayed undercover for so long, helping to mete out court decisions?

One of them said that he would reveal the secret of their mission. They had orders to capture the new Leader and take him back to Mars! They believed that he thought Martians were a cruel people, but it was not so, as they only wanted to find a safer place to live because they had been told that Mars was about to implode and come crashing about their heads.

The chairman of the judges spoke out, 'If you want us to believe that you are a peaceful people, then prove it. We are all astonished that we have had amongst us two Martians dressed up as we are for so long without our realising it, and I must commend you on your disguises. Come to think of it, you both always gave consenting judgements and never had anything of your own to add. That was very clever indeed!'

Realising that this was an attempt at flattery to put them off their guard, one of them said, 'We have to carry out our mission, and nothing you say will change that. We are going to leave you here, tied up, until you are found by the court officials, and meanwhile, we will have a head start to capture the Leader.'

The judges were astonished to hear of such a fantastic plan. How could they force their Leader to go along with them to Mars when he was so closely guarded? they asked themselves.

And then they realised with horror, so far as they were concerned, it was unfortunately a Friday night and that it couldn't be until Monday morning that the courts would reopen and they could then be released. On reflection, the Leader could look after himself; they had themselves to worry about!

They were all tied to their own judges' chairs, and the pair left the court building as normal, arousing no suspicions. The doorman, whose duty it was to lock up after they had all left, saw the two leave, and as they left, they told him that the others had gone out by the back door where their cars were. So thinking that everyone had left, he locked up and went home.

The first thing the pair had to do was to get themselves out of their judge disguise and into normal clothes. They'd left their own in the court anteroom in their rush to get out, so when they passed a clothes shop, they broke in and fitted themselves out in such a way that they wouldn't stand out from the crowd.

They made for the Leader's home as they knew that he wouldn't be working at the palace over the weekend. It had extensive grounds as you would expect, and the place was surrounded with high gates and railings which were no doubt protected with electricity, so it was not going to be easy to get in. On the other hand, they'd heard how, if you were lucky with your timing, you could get in through the drainage system of such places.

Ideally, this method was only to be used at night when hardly any drainage occurred, so they decided to find its outlet and lie low until the middle of the night. They then entered the drain by picking up the heavy cover and made their way along it, beneath the gates, until they reached where they thought must be the kitchens. There, they found an outside inspection chamber whose cover they pushed open and got out.

Next, they quietly broke in through the back door and hid in a hallway cupboard whilst they checked out the layout by taking turns to go and look around.

Eventually, they reached the first floor where the Leader and his wife had the main bedroom, and they both charged in, only to find it empty!

It had been kept a secret, as were all their movements, but this was the weekend when the Leader and his wife had been invited to stay in the countryside with old friends with the purpose, whilst there, of declaring a new factory open and visiting a performance together in the evening.

They'd taken several of their staff with them, of course, so that their own place had very few servants left behind, which is why the two found that they were able to simply walk out of the front door without being noticed and escape!

At least, they now knew the layout of the building for the time when they would come back to capture the Leader.

After the Leader and his wife returned with their staff, the two aliens made another attempt to capture him, as instructed. From what they had seen, there was no possibility of capturing him in the palace as it was so heavily guarded, so they decided to do it whilst he was out and about.

They found out from information on their transponder that he was due to make a presentation at a gathering out in the countryside. It was to be for some individuals who had recently rescued some cave explorers who had become trapped by unusual rising waters. They managed to mingle with the crowd, awaiting an opportunity, and they were lucky that when he left to go to the bathroom to freshen up after his journey, he was attended by only one court official.

They pounced on them and gave them both an injection, which shortly afterwards made them drowsy enough to be walked out through a side door, uncomplaining.

Making out as though they were drunk and partially hiding the Leader's face, they went to the skyport where they picked up the next flytaxi to Mars.

The Chief Martian, as he was called, was delighted that he would now have his hands on Jupiter's Leader. As soon as they landed, they were taken to him in his private mansion.

The Leader was given a room and made comfortable as the Chief intended to try to get his cooperation to allow all the Martians to go and live in Jupiter to escape their impending fate. How far he would succeed in his plan remained to be seen.

When he was refreshed, the Leader was asked to accompany an official to be presented to the Chief, and they made their way along corridors to a room which, having guards outside the door, was clearly the Chief's main room.

The Chief offered him refreshments and invited him to sit down, saying, 'It is always a pleasure meeting the head of another planet, and I extend to you the warmest of welcomes.

'I'll come straight to the point. We have a major problem here as our scientists tell us that they have observed clear signs that we are likely to implode at some point during the next ten years. We are told that there will be no warning, just that, without any previous sign, this whole planet will disintegrate, and with us in it!

'You can see why it is vital that we move out elsewhere in time, and I would like to explore with you the possibility of your planet accommodating us all. I know that, like here, you have vast wastelands which have been left undrained, and my proposal is that we could finance the drainage in return for your allowing us to build and live on the reclaimed areas. So what do you say? It would help your economy having us there, and we could all live safely side by side in peace.'

The Leader half expected this proposition and replied, 'First of all, I would like to thank you for your hospitality. Perhaps I could have come here to talk to you without being drugged and forced to come, but I quite understand why your operatives thought it was essential. Either way, that is in the past, and we can now examine your problem together without any ill feeling.

'We ourselves have been having problems of our own. We have men from Earth staying with us, and they tell us that their scientists are giving them similar warnings so that they too want to decamp to Jupiter.

'There simply isn't room for everyone here, but we have heard of a younger planet which has not yet been occupied, and this might be ideal for your purposes. I could make further enquiries if you like.'

The Chief was taken a bit aback by this suggestion. He had always believed that Jupiter would be most suitable as their second home, and here he was being offered some uninhabited planet instead! But maybe it was worth considering, he thought.

If earthmen and themselves were to be crowded into Jupiter with those already there and their planet itself might implode as it grew older, it could well be that the other planet was not such a bad option and worth looking into.

They could live there on their own without any need for clashes between the groups any longer. That would make a pleasant change, he thought.

'So how far away is this planet, and what do we know about it?' the Chief asked.

The Leader saw the possibility of finally disposing of their dreaded enemy to a faraway planet where they would not cause them any further trouble, so he expounded with fabricated information about it. It was quite a new planet, he said, so it would not implode for many generations. It had, he was told, many valuable minerals which could be mined near the surface without having to dig deep down, and its climate was said to be one of the most pleasant in the whole galaxy.

The Chief was normally of an enquiringly suspicious mind, but when he heard of all these wonderful attributes of a new homeland just lying there waiting to be occupied, he was unusually overcome and convinced, so he asked for the coordinates so he could take a party there to investigate it.

The Leader of Jupiter was sorely tempted to give the wrong details to the Chief so that he would be sent on a wasted journey and possibly die in the process, for after all, the Martians had been their worst enemies for generations. When he considered it more sensibly, however, there wouldn't be much point destroying one leader as another one would soon take over, and nothing much would have been achieved.

What worried him, however, was what would be his own fate if the Chief went there and came back having found that what he'd told him was a pack of lies. Somehow, he realised, he had to find a way to stop him going in the first place. Why on earth he'd thought up this pack of lies at all, he just couldn't imagine. He'd obviously not thought it through properly in the rush of deciding how to cope with the Chief's wish to settle in Jupiter.

What was he to do? And then it came to him how he could delay things. Suddenly, he fell to the ground, complaining of pains in his chest, and he was rushed off to the hospital for treatment. There, seeing who he was, the hospital authorities kept him in a private room under guard for observation for several days whilst he made a slow recovery, and no one was allowed to see him except his own aides.

The Chief was impatient and was keen to get on his way to the new planet, but he was not allowed to visit the Leader to get the coordinates for several days. He was furious with the delay but realised that he had to wait, as the information was known only to the Leader. And until he could get in to see him, he was forced to delay his trip.

Meanwhile, the Leader had a private visit from his trusted adviser, and he told him all about his quandary. He couldn't refuse to hand over the coordinates, and even if he did, the Chief could come back, and there was no knowing what he would do when he realised he'd been told a string of lies. There was no time to lose before the Chief was allowed to see him, so something had to be done quickly.

His adviser could always be relied on for solutions to problems the Leader found himself in from time to time, and this was not going to be an exception. He proposed that they either arrange to have him waylaid and killed or sent packing back to Mars.

That sounded rather drastic, and in any case, the second alternative didn't seem sensible as he could return in force and dispose of the Leader and indeed his subjects with him. The problem was even more exacerbated by the fact that if the Chief disappeared in Jupiter in mysterious circumstances, his followers would all be there like a shot, searching for him and causing their usual mayhem, similar to the sorties from Mars they'd experienced previously.

There was only one alternative. He had to suffer an accident which would prevent him going on such a journey, but not one that was life-threatening, of course. How was this to be arranged? they wondered. Then it came to them.

He'd had a long-standing arrangement to meet some of Jupiter's judges to try to get a better system of justice in Mars and thought that they might give him some useful pointers. The meeting was known about by the Leader's adviser because he'd been invited along as well on behalf of the Leader. He usually took an interest in meetings with foreigners, and if he couldn't attend for some reason, the adviser always stood in for him and then reported back.

By knowing where the Chief would be, they concocted a plan between them which involved secretly engaging a member of the underworld. He or she would be present at the entrance to the courts, and as the Chief climbed the steps, he would be 'accidentally' pushed against by the other one rushing by, and he would be sent tumbling down to the bottom, hopefully breaking one of his spindly legs in the process. They also had a plan B which involved a similar confrontation elsewhere if required.

The operative to be chosen for the job was to be left to the adviser to decide as usual. That was part of the work he was expected to do. He contacted an ex-prisoner who knew a number of reliable shady characters, and it didn't take long to set up the planned 'accident'. He was called in for the purpose and was given all the details of his instructions.

It couldn't have worked better. One moment, the Chief was climbing the steps to go in, and the next moment, this idiot came rushing past him, knocking him off his feet, and he fell all the way back down the stairs. Sure enough, his spindly legs couldn't take the fall on the hard surface, and he screamed out as one of them broke. An ambulance was soon on the scene, making him comfortable, and he was taken off to the nearest hospital as planned.

The adviser was informed of the success of the operation, and he, in turn, put a short call through to the Leader, simply saying, 'Plan B isn't needed.' He knew, by this, that his worries were over for the present, at least.

The Leader soon showed the physiotherapists at his hospital that he was fit to be released, and he promptly returned with his adviser to his Jupiter palace to resume his duties whilst the Mars Chief continued to recover slowly in hospital from his major trauma.

As to the Chief's condition, it transpired that the damage to his leg was thought to be more severe than at first thought, and the specialist told him that because of this, and if all went well, he might eventually be able to walk a little but that he certainly couldn't undertake long intergalactic space journeys for a very long time as the effort would prove too much for his legs. And he might well end up being a permanent cripple if he tried such foolishness.

The Leader's adviser made discreet enquiries about the prognosis for the Chief's recovery and conveyed the good news to the Leader. At least they'd allowed him to live this way, they consoled their consciences!

With this dreadful news, the Chief realised that unless he was foolish enough to undertake the journey home despite the medical advice, he would be forced to live out his days in Jupiter. Then he told himself, in his usual positive way, that the main thing was to be able to recover sufficiently to get out of the hospital. What he would be able to do afterwards would have to remain to be seen.

CHAPTER TWENTY-FOUR

By this time, the Leader's eldest son, Stefan, had grown up and, at the age of eighteen, was generally expected to follow in his father's footsteps and take over ruling Jupiter when the right time came.

The problem with Stefan was that he'd grown up to be a bit of a rebel. It was probably due to the influence of his friends, whose parents were so occupied with advancing themselves in Jupiter's society that they spent very little time with their children and neglected their upbringing.

Being left to their own devices and knowing that who they were meant that they could get away with any escapade they thought would amuse them, they often went over the borderline between honest and dishonest activity, which led to them being highlighted in the Jupiter journals as being worthless characters.

Stefan was kept more strictly as he grew up because the Leader's staff, especially one female who had a particular liking for him, tried their best to keep him on the right side of the law, but since he was often away with his dubious friends, their ability to groom him in the right way was limited.

On one or two occasions, it became necessary, with bribery, to save Stefan from the clutches of the law when he had stupidly joined in with his friends on an illegal enterprise, which they thought would be fun and exciting, only to find that the whole thing went wrong, and they were all caught at it and arrested.

So it was with this background that Stefan got to hear about the Chief from Mars having been hospitalised with his broken leg. This was an important person, and it seemed to him that it would be fun to see if he could break through all the security and get to see him. It would be a great feather in his cap amongst all the lesser-quality escapades his friends had previously thought up and indulged in.

How would he go about it, and if he managed to succeed, what would he say to him? Maybe there was something he could think of that his father had overlooked, and it would put him back in his good books. As he'd grown older, he'd begun to realise that if he was to take over and become the Leader one day, he'd better start behaving much more responsibly.

But this opportunity simply couldn't be missed. It was like being able to get to see a king without permission, except here, being the Leader's son, there would be no repercussions if things went wrong. He half wondered, however, if it was so exciting an idea anyway as it would have been different if he wasn't who he was. But then again, he thought his friends wouldn't, hopefully, look at it that way and be amazed at his temerity.

Stefan had developed a certain air about him as he'd grown up, which made those in his company feel that he was a person of authority. He decided to use this to his advantage. He bought a white gown and a stethoscope from a medical supplies shop by pretending that he had just qualified as a medical specialist in the field of surgery.

They were quite impressed with him in the shop because being the Leader's son, they thought it admirable that he was taking up a profession whilst he waited until the time came for him to take over as Leader. The experience would give him a deeper understanding of what normal lives were like when it came to his turn to rule, they thought when he'd left, and they chatted about his visit.

Stefan discovered exactly where the Chief was laid up, so he arrived there and boldly marched into the hospital, wearing his specialist's outfit. He squiggled his name on the register as he smartly walked past security, and as he wore a false moustache, he wasn't recognised by any of the staff as he made his way to the Chief's room.

By then, it was mid-morning, and the usual daily formalities of food and bodily measurements had been completed. The Chief's specialist was due to visit him some time during the day anyway, and so when Stefan walked in, he assumed it was him at first, but then exclaimed, 'You're not my surgeon. Who are you?'

Stefan said, 'No, your highness. I am the Leader's son Stefan. I wanted to come and see you to talk about Mars, and I thought it best to disguise myself. Otherwise, I knew you're not allowed visitors, and I couldn't get in.

The Chief was quite taken aback. He'd never met the Leader's son, so he had no way of recognising him. Nevertheless, Stefan's getting into his room was a shock because he thought he was safe from unwanted visitors, but Stefan pointed out to him that it was only because he was the Leader's son that nobody had objected.

This put the Chief's mind at rest, and he started unfolding the story of his unfortunate mishap on the steps when he broke his leg and how he had been told that it was likely that he would never again be able to return on the long journey to his homeland—Mars.

Stefan saw this as a great opportunity to prove to his father how clever he was. This could well put him back in his good books once and for all. He asked the Chief if the operation had been successful, and he said that his leg felt good and that the physiotherapists had told him that they were very pleased with his progress and they'd got him walking a little.

Stefan said, 'In that case, Your Honour, I can see no reason why you can't return to Mars after all, and if you like, I will accompany you there and make all the arrangements. I'm quite sure that there'll be no problem with your doing the journey because you can come in the special spacecraft which my father recently gave me. It achieves speeds far in excess of the usual ones, and it will be a pleasure to do this for you. We'll be there quite quickly, and I'm sure you'll be all right.

The Chief was beginning to realise that what he had been told about not being able to get back to Mars was just a ruse by the Leader to delay having to cooperate over the Martians moving into the uninhabited planet—here, he had the Leader's son offering to undo his own father's plan. Not only that, he realised, the Leader's son was proposing to put himself in the Chief's hands by accompanying him back there!

Maybe by accepting Stefan's offer, he could deny the success the Leader thought he'd achieved by detaining him unnecessarily. He'd go along with Stefan's idea and see what to do about the Leader afterwards, he decided.

'How do we get out without any query?' he asked Stefan.

'Oh, that's easy,' Stefan replied. 'We will get an orderly to move you into a wheelchair, and I will push you out of the building to my flycar, saying that you'd been told that some fresh air would do you good. From there, we can soon be at the spaceport where my special spacecraft will be piloted back to Mars, and you can then finish recuperating in your own home. How does that sound?'

The Chief thought it was too good to be true. There he had been lying in hospital in Jupiter one moment, wondering how long he'd have to stay there, and the next he was going home to Mars accompanied by the eldest son of his arch-enemy, Jupiter's Leader, innocently putting himself in his clutches! *What could be better?* he thought.

So they put the plan into action. He was wheeled out by this apparent specialist straight past security and then driven to the spaceport where they both boarded the spacecraft. The journey was uneventful except for how quickly it was completed, and they landed at Mars, where the Chief was wheeled out by Stefan who, by then, had decided to dispense with the moustache.

On their way to his palace, the Chief told Stefan how indebted he was to him and that, when they arrived, he would show him round personally and generally be the perfect host. He said he hoped he wouldn't rush back as there was so much to see, if he had the time, that was.

When they arrived, the Chief invited Stefan into the palace and sat him down with refreshments. He then got himself wheeled into another private room where he sent an immediate message to the Jupiter Leader that he was now back after all and that he had his eldest son with him. He didn't actually use the word *hostage*, but the Leader knew what he meant. He realised that he was going to have to reveal where the uninhabited planet was after all if he wanted his son back in one piece, thanks to his foolishness!

What a stupid son he had! The phrase kept going through his head. If only he had explained to him all the politics surrounding these major world problems, it might have been different. It wouldn't have taken long.

Earth was likely to collapse eventually and Mars with it, and if Jupiter was to remain solely for its own people, the other two had to fight over the one uninhabited planet. He should have also explained all this and that as time passed, these problems had become more and more pressing, needing an early solution.

Through his son's stupid showing off, the dynamics of these different political pressures had become even more intricate, and if he was to save him from being used as a pawn in this game of chess, he was going to have to use all the ingenuity he had in order to save him as well. That was all he needed on top of all his other problems, he thought.

For the present, Stefan didn't realise that he was not going to be allowed to return to Jupiter. The Chief secretly ordered Stefan's special spacecraft to be impounded awaiting his further orders, and Stefan was shown around the sights of the capital during the day and the nightlife afterwards, feeling that he was just a tourist, but an important one, of course. They had front seats at events and the best tables at restaurants, all at the Chief's expense.

One day, soon afterwards, Stefan wanted to leave the room he had been given in the palace, and he found, to his horror, that the door was locked and there was a guard outside, preventing him from leaving. This was the first indication he had that something had gone wrong.

He asked to see the Chief but was told that he was too busy. He tried telephoning him but to no avail. He started to get quite desperate. Why was this happening to him, the important son of Jupiter's Leader? What had he got himself involved in? he wondered.

He then realised that he still had his transponder with him, so he contacted his father in Jupiter, telling him what was happening to him. You can imagine the fury with which the Leader took the call. His own son had upset all his political plans simply by showing off childishly, and it took all the restraint he could muster to talk to him calmly. He knew that the call was probably being intercepted so he had to be cautious how they spoke, so he simply asked if he was well and hoped to see him soon.

This wasn't much consolation for Stefan, and he realised that if he was going to be able to escape, it would require a great deal of ingenuity on his part. He'd never been much good at thinking for himself as everything had always been done for him. Just as he was wondering what to do, the door was unlocked, and a maid came in with some food. She was quite a young alien girl and very pretty in her way.

It dawned on him that she had the key to his door, having let herself in. He didn't expect her to cooperate willingly in his escape, so he saw no alternative but to muffle her mouth with one of the pillowcases and tie her to the bed whilst he took her keys from her.

He told her he wasn't going to hurt her, but she still wanted to scream out for help but found that she couldn't. And not wanting him to pay any more attention to her, she decided to remain quiet whilst she watched what he was going to do.

He looked out of the window, but being high up, he decided there was no escape that way. It would have been different if he'd been an athlete. He might have scrambled along the parapet and worked his way down to the ground that way.

So he turned his attention to the guard on the door. For his part, he knew the girl had gone in with the food but was still inside. He'd seen when she had gone in but began wondering if she was in any sort of trouble in there as it seemed to be too long for her just to have left his tray.

Stefan hid behind the door as the guard came in to check, and as he got inside, Stefan pounced on him, taking him by surprise and managing to disarm him. He tied him up as well after taking his uniform off him and putting it on himself. The fit was almost perfect, so he saw it as his passport out of there.

He knew the town sufficiently from having been shown around, so he had a pretty good idea where the spaceport was. All he had to do was to find a way to get there!

The uniform helped a great deal because as he marched out, indicating he was just going out for a smoke, he received a smile and a gesture showing that whoever saw him hadn't the faintest idea who he really was—that is, all except one!

He was quite friendly with Stefan's guard. And whilst recognising the guard's badges upon his lapels, the face didn't fit, and he knew something was wrong, and he'd better follow in case his friend had been harmed.

Stefan went over to where the flycars were parked and commandeered one of them as it had been left open with the key in it. As he drove off, the other guard followed him, but Stefan spotted him in time and flew off at speed, leaving the other helpless as he only had an ordinary vehicle which didn't fly. All he could do was to send in a report of his suspicions.

The authorities, hearing what had happened, issued instructions for those on duty at the spaceport to be ultra cautious and to look out for Stefan's arrival, telling them he was wearing a guard's uniform and that they were not to be fooled by it.

Stefan had enough sense to know that they'd be on the lookout for someone wearing this identifiable uniform, so he went into a shop on his way and bought some ordinary clothes, saying he'd just come off-duty and fancied something new to wear.

He'd been given a small amount of their local currency by the Chief in case he wanted something whilst in Mars without having to ask for money each time he might want to buy something, and it was with this money that he bought his new outfit. He put it on in the changing room, parcelling up the uniform which he took with him in case he could use it.

When he arrived at the spaceport, he went in with a group of tourists who were on a tour as part of their package holiday. On their way round the exhibits, he spotted his own spacecraft which, for some reason, had been left quite near the open doors, probably because the place had been full when it was brought in.

He noticed that no one seemed to be specially guarding it as they had been instructed to do, and he quickly concluded that this must be because they had locked away its starter key, thinking they'd disabled it that way.

He always kept on his key ring a small device which, with its ray, could be used to start the spacecraft without a key, so he slipped away from the group and hid until they'd left. The place was then empty, so he zapped the device, the cockpit section opened, and he was inside like a shot.

But maybe they had disabled the ship to prevent it from flying! He quickly ran through the controls and found them to be intact, to his great relief. He drove the spaceship outside and, without further ado, took off, and his craft took him fast out of Mars's orbit and on his way back home at last.

Never again would he do stupid things involving space without discussing the full implications with someone who knew all the ins and outs of what he had in mind. And he certainly wouldn't try to show off in front of his mates ever again, he decided. He'd grown out of all that showing off, he thought.

He'd reached about three-quarters of the way back to Jupiter when an almighty battle broke out. The Martians and the Jupiterians were at each other's throats again, with their spacecrafts zooming all over the place with gunfire and lasers shooting everywhere. Stefan was just beginning to think he'd been lucky to get out of it all alive when a Martian spacecraft spotted him and decided to shoot him down.

It was only because his craft had its unusual extra speed facility that he was able to dodge the gunfire and laser shots directed at him, and by a smart manoeuvre, he was able to come up behind his attacker and destroy it instead. It left a colourful streak in the atmosphere as he watched it fall back on to Mars, strangely enough just missing the presidential palace as the wreckage landed.

The battle raged for days, on and off, and Stefan knew that if he didn't get back to Jupiter soon, he would run out of fuel. He couldn't hide anywhere out in space and luckily, and out of desperation, came upon the idea of trying to attach himself to one of the Jupiterian spaceships. He had heard that this had been successfully achieved before, so he had nothing to lose by trying it himself.

He chose one that looked suitable for the purpose and, using his transponder, communicated with its captain, who agreed to his idea, realising who he was. He docked beside it, thus presenting to the enemy the appearance of a giant flying machine with enhanced firing power. When they spotted it, the Martians thought that they'd better withdraw and return to Mars rather than take on this behemoth of a spacecraft. After all, they could always return to the fight when they'd built a few of their own to match.

The captain of the attached spacecraft invited Stefan in, seeing that he knew him to be the son of the Leader, and thought it might do himself some good to show him some hospitality. So he began making his way through the portal, leaving his own craft on automatic pilot, which he was able to direct from his transponder whilst on his visit.

As he was just about to enter the other spacecraft, a Martian craft flew perilously close to both of them in error, causing pressure waves to rock the passageway almost to breaking point, but somehow, the two craft held together long enough for Stefan to scramble through into the other one. The two machines managed to stay attached, so Stefan could always get back.

The captain of the other spacecraft called himself Trem and introduced himself to Stefan. He said, 'Welcome to my humble spacecraft. Can I get you anything to eat or drink? And how is your father? I have never had the honour to meet him. I was awarded a medal for bravery, but it was presented by his sister as he was away on another engagement, although he did take the trouble to send a message congratulating me.

Stefan replied, 'Thank you for allowing me to dock beside your craft. It made a great difference to me as I got heavily involved in the dogfight that took place out there, and I am indebted to you, Trem, for my life. I will certainly tell my father how you helped me when I needed it most, and I am sure he will see you personally this time when he gives you another award.'

Trem was astonished to receive such praise. After all, Stefan had invited himself!

Before Stefan could return to his spacecraft, another Martian decided to make a last-minute surprise attack, but Trem's crew were ever vigilant and, seeing it coming, gave it a blast of infrared rays, which set it on fire, and they watched it as it fell like a stone through the atmosphere.

Stefan decided to get away as soon as possible in case another attack took place, and fortunately, all the remaining Martian craft had been ordered back to base, so his remaining journey turned out to be uneventful after all.

His father, the Leader, just didn't know what to make of his son. On the one hand, he had stupidly allowed himself to be taken off to Mars by the Chief, but on the other, he had shown great resourcefulness in escaping his clutches and even arriving back intact through one of the worst air battles the two sides had ever embarked upon.

He certainly intended rewarding Trem for the part he played in his son's rescue flight and asked his aide to find out when his tour of duty was due to finish so he could arrange the investiture personally, as his son had promised.

When he heard about how his son had thought up the linking of the two craft and how doing so seemed to have repelled the Martian attack, the Leader ordered the main manufacturers to come up with a similar double-sized spaceship with interlocking capabilities and speed. That would keep them at bay, he thought, and how clever his son had been to think of it. Maybe, after all, he could safely pass over the reins to him when it was his time to retire.

CHAPTER TWENTY-FIVE

· · · · · · ● · · · · · · ·

The alien Yost suddenly wondered where his friend Zooba was. A lot of events had occurred since he'd last seen him, and because he had been so good to him, he still felt concerned about his welfare.

Upon making enquiries, he was informed that Zooba, having experienced such hair-raising excitement, had decided to hand over his judgebot business and retire. Nevertheless, he was not one for remaining idle and still had all his wits about him, so he thought he would seek an advisory position with Jupiter's main chemical warfare business, which was how Yost was able to track him down, public records being so accessible.

Yost made an appointment to see him, and when he went in, he was so excited to see him again. Zooba told him of the events which had occurred between the Martians and themselves, and Yost said that he'd seen some of the dogfights between the two warring sides for himself and wondered if Zooba thought anything could be done finally to bring matters to a head and resume a more peaceful existence between the two planets.

Zooba said that this was why he had joined the company, hoping to devise such a dreadful deterrent that the Martians would put aside their animosity and concentrate on their main objective, which was to find themselves another planet to decamp to before disaster struck Mars and they would all perish.

He told Yost in secret confidence that the company was on the verge of a completely new discovery. They had been ordered by the Leader to pull out all the stops, and they'd finally succeeded. It only remained for a few more trials before it could be used. After all, he said, they had to make sure that it could be made safe to handle by whoever was to use it.

Yost said that he didn't want to pry but asked Zooba how it worked, as he was most interested. Zooba replied that he was not sure of all its intricacies but he'd been told that it was a most effective weapon. It involved the use of several components, each of which was deadly in its own right but, combined, formed the most powerful weapon ever devised.

Zooba took Yost from his office down to where this monster was being created, and Yost was astonished at its size. It filled nearly a quarter of the room, and Yost logically enquired, given its size, how it could be deployed.

Zooba explained that they were now miniaturising the whole thing so that it could be fitted inside one of their new double-sized spaceships. This was delaying finalising it, but once achieved, there would be no other weapon like it.

Yost wanted to know, in his simple way, why it was thought necessary to invent such a weapon, and he was told that the Martians were expected to try to invade Jupiter again at any time, with the intention this time of throwing them all out. This could not be allowed to happen, and so this monstrous weapon had been created.

They were sending a message to one of their contacts in Mars, which they knew would be intercepted, revealing the existence of this new weapon in the hope that it would make them decide not to invade, and they hoped that it would do the trick and make them look elsewhere, such as the uninhabited planet that had already been mentioned as an option.

Yost thanked Zooba for trusting him with this information and returned to his spaceship.

When the information about the new weapon reached the Chief in Mars, he had his doubts as to whether it really existed because it sounded so lethal, and he simply had to find out for certain if it was true. So much depended on it.

Utilising one of the regular trading spaceships travelling between the two planets, he despatched a trusted envoy under the cover of being one of its crew, standing in at the last minute because one of their number had been taken ill. All trading ships were preauthorised to pass through the portal in the veil by electronic means, so no undue delays occurred, whichever way one was travelling.

Naturally, the Chief also had his spies everywhere in Jupiter just as the Leader had his in Mars, so it wasn't long before corroboration came through that this giant of a weapon actually existed. But what it consisted of, the Chief needed to know.

One of his spies had worked his way up undercover through the war factory over a period, as instructed, which gave him access to the plans for the new weapon, but as the scientists hadn't yet achieved the necessary miniaturisation, the Martian Chief was still unable to learn exactly what his force would be faced with in an all-out war.

He didn't dare take a chance on such an important matter, so he decided to hold back the attack until he could be more certain about it. This gave a window of opportunity to the Leader to make the first strike, but he, in turn, wasn't sure of the Chief's intentions and, in any case, wasn't ready himself, so there was a virtual stalemate until either side was prepared to make the first move.

The Chief instructed his spy to let him know how the final stages of preparing the Leader's new device for war was progressing, but out of the blue, the individual was dismissed from the company on suspicion of selling its secrets, an offence against the planet's security laws.

The Leader had got wind of this from one of his own operatives who had been keeping a watchful eye on the undercover one for some time and had noticed that he had been acting strangely by looking into and unusually constantly asking others in the workforce about their progress on the project.

This sudden development put the Chief at a distinct disadvantage. Without his spy in the factory any longer, he had no way of knowing the details of the new weapon, so essential to his knowing how best to attack. Maybe, after all, it would be sensible to take the advantage of making the first strike, but on the other hand, he could lose the battle by doing so, he feared.

Whilst the Chief was mulling over his options about what would be best for his planet, Jupiter's Leader was getting reports that an attack had been launched on some remote hamlets in the south of the main occupied region of his planet. His spies there reported that a number of Martians had arrived suddenly and had taken over the place, ejecting the occupants into the street.

It transpired, through subsequent information, that the Chief's son had taken things into his own hands and had launched an attack on Jupiter, not knowing anything about the new weapon and thinking, like the Leader's son had done, that he would show off his future powers of leadership. He'd obviously forgotten all about how he had been told that, through the Leader's son's stupidity, it had led him into becoming the Chief's virtual hostage.

Even though the miniature version of the new weapon wasn't yet ready, the Leader decided to deploy a platoon to take the large version to the area that was under attack, and they set off as soon as they could.

It wasn't long before they arrived just outside the attacked area, and their General weighed up his options carefully. He decided to place the weapon high up on a hillside overlooking and pointing directly at the hamlet so that the enemy Martians could see it clearly. If that didn't deter them and make them depart, he didn't know what would.

His adjutant then suggested that they should send a salvo over the hamlets during daylight so that the enemy could see the strength of their firepower, and the General agreed.

The effect was astonishing. As the main salvo flew across the area, the Martians saw that smaller incendiaries shot out of it and landed on several of the dwellings, setting them on fire. They came running out in a panic and made for their spacecrafts, only to find that they too had been burnt up in the conflagration. They ran around helplessly and were soon rounded up and taken in as prisoners back to the main town for interrogation.

When the Leader heard what a remarkable effect the new weapon had, he was more determined than ever to get it into a miniature state so it could be used to take the battle to Mars and finish the endless fight off once and for all.

· · · · · · · · · · ● · · · · · · · · · ·

The Chief had a complete change of heart once he'd found out about the devastating ability of Jupiter's remarkable new weapon. He knew he had nothing that could touch it in firepower, and it would take ages to get hold of its plans and make copies, not that this would solve the problem since there would be an impasse because of the fact that neither side would then have a superior weapon to achieve victory.

He decided to contact the Leader in Jupiter, and he told him that he had no belligerent intentions towards Jupiter. He had decided that their best bet for ultimate survival was to descend on Earth and live there instead. Earth would last longer than Jupiter, he said, and it made sense to go there instead of disturbing Jupiter's population. There was no mention of Jupiter's powerful weapon, of course!

Naturally, the Leader was delighted to hear this. Whether he could trust his word after all that had gone before remained to be seen.

But he couldn't help being concerned about Earth. Should he let them know what he had just been told, he wondered, or let them find out for themselves? It could be fortuitous to gain goodwill if he were to tell them, and perhaps it was a golden opportunity to establish a future colony there themselves in case of need by appearing to be cooperative and tipping them off. So he decided to let them know Mars's intentions.

CHAPTER TWENTY-SIX

· · · · · · ●●● ● ●●● · · · · · ·

The Leader of Jupiter accordingly contacted Yost, who happened to be on his way back there anyway, and asked him to come to see him in the palace as soon as he'd landed.

As they sat together and the Leader confided in him all about the previous events, Yost said that he was not in the least surprised at the Martians' change of heart as he had seen for himself how lethal the new weapon was.

He wondered to himself, but didn't say so, if Earth would be able to resist a Martian onslaught even without this weapon, and remembering his close friendship with Zooba, he really didn't want anything untoward to happen to him.

They both agreed that Yost would go straight to Zooba and let him know all about the impending threat from Mars. Zooba, in turn, could advise the British prime minister and the US president, and they could decide on the best plan of action between them.

Yost set off for Earth, and as he approached and passed through the portal, he contacted Zooba for an appointment to visit him. He told Zooba that it was nothing to worry about as there was no point in frightening him about the impending invasion until he saw him and something sensible could be decided upon.

Once they were together, however, he told him everything, including the possibility of Jupiter allowing Earth to use the new weapon. Of course, he would have to arrange it with the Leader but didn't see any major problem on that score.

Zooba thought otherwise. How were they to transport this enormous weaponry through space to Earth, he wondered.

Yost replied that if the Leader agreed to the proposition in principle, he could see no reason why, once it had the plans, Earth couldn't make its own copy of the weapon.

He went on to say that he was willing to return to Jupiter and plead with the Leader to allow it. But what could he offer in return? he wondered. It wouldn't appeal to the Leader to give away his secret weapon without some satisfactory deal in return, he said enquiringly.

The Leader thought long and hard, but it didn't take much initiative to conclude in the end that the best return they could want would be to be welcomed to live on Earth themselves if it ever became essential, and this was his reply.

Yost decided that this arrangement needed to be concluded between the two great leaders rather than by himself, so he contacted the UK prime minister in the Jupiter's Leader's presence, and he, in turn, discussed it with the US president.

The two Earth leaders soon saw a way forward and concluded that they, and other Earth countries, could make space for the fleeing aliens from Jupiter if it became absolutely necessary to do so. At least by promising this, they could be sure of getting their hands on the plans of Jupiter's world-beating invention.

So the deal was done. Global warming had, by this time, made more land available to accommodate those from Jupiter, contrary to the belief that it caused the oceans to rise and reduce it.

The Dutch nation had originally shown the way to extend their territory out to sea with polders, where most of west Holland was under the sea. And the idea had been enhanced in the intervening decades by engineers finding a way to raise levels above what had gone before, so there was plenty of scope for aliens to clear the way and live side by side with Man on Earth without too much disruption. You only had to look at what the Middle Eastern countries had achieved by building out into the sea and even over deserts.

The deal having been done and duly officially recorded, a copy of the plans was despatched by specially chartered spaceship and delivered to the BT Tower in London, where the prime minister's PMG group had its base.

This was seen as quite an achievement because the Chief's operatives in Mars had, by monitoring all space messages, heard all about the deal and had informed him about it.

It was very concerning for him because it meant that unless he could invade before the great weapon had been constructed, he had very little chance of doing so afterwards. He'd heard enough about its capabilities not to ignore it and started to wonder how he could manufacture one for himself.

Indeed, he thought, what if he simply informed Earth or let it slip out that he'd completed several miniature versions of the weapon which were already installed in spaceships, ready for the attack. Maybe that's all that would be necessary for Earth to surrender without a fight, he thought.

Close contact was kept by officials from both Jupiter and Earth about the plan, and it soon became apparent that the miniaturisation of the weapon was not going to be an easy task. They also realised that anyone saying differently was either a remarkable engineer or a liar.

The problem was to find a way to install sufficient firepower in a small space. The large version had enough room to contain the satellite discharges which were so lethal when it exploded but not so with the smaller version.

Maybe a halfway could be invented, which would still cause sufficient disruption to turn the tide of battle. These were the thoughts of the engineers on each planet as they struggled with the dilemma of proving that they could come up with the answer before the others could.

·········●·········

Meanwhile, preparations had to be made ready in the US and the UK to deal with an alien landing. Other countries were advised to be prepared, but their own tactics were left to them to organise, although they were expected to report any sightings or landings to the PMG group in the BT Tower in London.

The prime minister reminded his group that any enemy attack had first to get through the portal, and there was no way they could do that without tipping them off that they were coming. He went on to say that even if they couldn't force their way through the portal, they would have a very long circuitous journey to seek out where the veil still remained to be completed and could well run out of fuel in the process.

As the Martian force, made up of several spaceships, approached the veil and its portal, they adopted a disguise they'd invented which made their spaceships take on the appearance of the regular trading ships. But when they arrived at the portal, seeking entry, they were denied access because the advanced security monitors saw through the disguise with radio beams and saw the spaceships for what they were.

Alarm bells rang out and lights flashed, indicating an emergency. Reserve security forces were quickly rushed to the spot, only to find that the Martian force had turned back with orders to get back as quickly as possible. The Chief was not prepared to lose his force in a fight at the portal platform but preferred to reconsider his tactics. Something more subtle was needed.

It came to him that if he could install an operative in the force which guarded the portal, he could well find a way of sabotaging their security from within, ultimately letting the main force through intact.

The security force was composed of carefully chosen men from Earth, so it would be very difficult for one of his people to infiltrate and work undercover. But nothing was impossible, he thought optimistically.

Then again, there was always the perennial possibility of bribery achieving his objective. But what would it take to persuade a human to turn on his own people? he wondered. He'd never tried it before, but what was there to lose? He might find that he'd lose an operative, but he'd done that before and was still in power, he reminded himself!

It kept going through his mind that Jupiter was known to be bigger than all the other planets put together and should therefore be capable of coming up with a useful solution.

By pure chance, a vacancy had arisen amongst the portal guards because one of them had been taken ill unexpectedly after suffering a fall. The protocol was that in such an event, the vacancy had to be filled immediately. Normally, they kept a couple of reserves in hand, but owing to it being a holiday period, they were forced to ask for volunteers to man the vacancy until things got back to normal.

Getting to hear of this and adopting a carefully made human disguise, the Chief himself decided to infiltrate the portal to let his troops through in order to attack Earth. It was far too important to leave it to anyone else to get it wrong.

The portal commander had his suspicions during the interview for the post. He didn't seem to quite get the right responses about the Chief's military background as they were somewhat vague. On the other hand, he was impressed with his demeanour and came to the conclusion that given that there were no other suitable applicants at the time, he would take him on, giving orders afterwards to the others to watch this newcomer carefully.

Despite all his foreknowledge of events and the latest information gleaned from his listening devices, the Chief simply had no idea that the opening of the portal was controlled by inserting a special code. He just assumed that an operative pressed a button and the whole thing opened up. How wrong he was!

It was not until whilst watching its operation that he saw the gatekeeper of the day go into the cabin and seem to do something with his computer, which then opened the portal up to the extent necessary only to accommodate what was actually being allowed through.

Different vehicles naturally had different sizes, and the computer measured them remotely after the insertion of the code began the process, so designed so as not to let any extra small items slip through at the same time without permission.

The operatives had been required to memorise the code lest it get into the wrong hands, but it seemed that one of the previous ones, in the flurry of having to check a whole convoy of several vehicles at once, had forgotten it and had needed to look it up and had then written it on the desk for convenience.

The Chief thought that if he could only get into the cabin, he might find something useful, not knowing, of course, that the key to the whole problem was already written on the desk! He knew that he had to get in there, so he devised a simple scheme. Just as the daily operative was leaving, the Chief, who had been hiding behind a pillar, jumped on him and dragged him back inside.

The Chief bound him up and demanded to know the code. The operative knew that it costs more than his life was worth to divulge it, but then, just as things were getting fraught between them, a latecomer spaceship arrived, requesting entry through the portal. The Chief thought quickly and released the operative just enough to let him work the entry system.

As he did so, the Chief, who was watching him very closely, noticed that he glanced at the desk, double-checking something. And when he looked at what it was, he saw that it was a code. No way could it be other than the so-called secret code, and he became even more convinced when the operative checked it more than once as he entered it in the computer.

Having finally found what he'd searched for, he decided that the operative was superfluous to his needs, so he dragged him outside. Checking that nobody was watching, he simply tipped the unfortunate operative over the edge to await his fate as he fell through space screaming.

Some of the operatives, on their way home, thought that they heard a scream, but not being able to see anything when they looked, they just went on their way, looking forward to their evening meal.

The way was now clear for the Chief to rally his invasion group, so he ordered them to gather outside the portal, and he would let them in. A few of them were amazed that their very own Chief had got himself in charge of the portal. No wonder he had remained their leader for so many years, they thought.

The moment came when the Chief had to operate the opening system, so he entered the code, but nothing happened! The portal stayed steadfastly closed! *How could this be?* he wondered. He tried again and again, entering the digits individually very carefully, but with the same result! Was there anything he could do about it, he wondered.

Then it dawned on him. The code must have been changed. How right he was! The system had an inbuilt security feature which changed the code from time to time without warning, supplying the operative with the new one on a printout which could come in at any time, replacing the old one.

This had happened that very day, just before the portal closed down, and the operative had put it in his pocket for use the next day, and certainly not to be left lying around overnight.

The very code the Chief needed to open up the portal was now winging its way down through space in the unfortunate official's pocket, and he was right back where he started! If only he'd known it was there, all would have gone smoothly, but how was he to have known? he asked himself.

Outside, his troops waited for the portal to open, but nothing happened. Eventually, they became impatient, realising that something was wrong, so they radioed the Chief to enquire about it. He told them that there was obviously a malfunction with it, and they had all better return back to Mars as there was no other way of opening it.

Before they left, one of them wondered about attacking the portal to force their way through it, but the Chief told him to forget the idea as he'd heard that the whole structure had become impregnable when further enhancements had recently been instituted. So they all left as instructed and returned to Mars to await further orders.

· · · · · · · · · ● ● · · · · · · · · · ·

On its way back to Jupiter, a spaceship was approaching the portal when, suddenly, a body went flying past. The captain made out that the body was in the uniform normally worn by the portal guards and decided to swoop down, and he managed to catch it in its extendable netting. He was unconscious when he was brought in but soon recovered under the captain's personal care.

When he gave details of what had happened to him, the captain was aghast. When he heard who had done it, he felt it his duty to notify everyone he thought ought to know. He asked the official if he felt up to opening the portal to let him out, and being so grateful that he had saved his life, he readily agreed. The spaceship then arrived at the portal, and using the latest code from his pocket, he let them pass through, much to their relief.

The spaceship landed at the spaceport in Jupiter, by which time the Leader had received the message of what had befallen the official. He thought it abominable that the Chief could have thrown the official out into space, facing the horror of certain death, and resolved there and then to enjoy a suitable reprisal against the Chief of Mars.

When they got to hear of it, those on Earth were thankful that the Martians hadn't broken through the portal, and the prime minister stepped up the security there by sacking all the officials instantly and posting them elsewhere. At the same time, he installed carefully vetted new ones.

He realised that by doing this, he was using a hammer to crack a nut, but it ensured that as far as possible, the portal would remain impregnable in the future and would protect Earth from further attack.

CHAPTER TWENTY-SEVEN

· · · · · ● ● ● ● ● ● ● ● ● ● ● · · · · ·

Great progress was being made in the specialist factory where the new weapon was being developed from the plans, especially in making smaller versions of it, and it was not long before their work was complete.

The prime minister relayed the good news to the US president who told him that in his view, the only way Mars would stop its belligerent attitude towards Earth, and indeed Jupiter, would be to launch an attack and give them a demonstration of the enormous firepower which the new weapon commanded.

Anyone undertaking the task would need to have their wits about them and be bold enough to take the fight to Mars, he said, and he added that he wondered if the prime minister, or indeed any other country, had a suitable candidate to carry out such an important task to save the future of the planet.

Meanwhile, the prime minister said he would make suitable enquiries and would call him back with any suggestions. Not wanting to waste time, he instructed the factory manager to get his people on to finding a way to be able to discharge the weapon in space without it destroying the spaceship deploying it. He was concerned that the blast created by the weapon could disable the spaceship beyond recovery, causing unnecessary loss of life.

They told him that it was a tall order, but they would do their best to find the answer. After much trial and error, the way was found. The weapon would be encased in hardened boron alloy so that this would give just enough time for the spacecraft to depart from the scene before the explosion took place.

Basil and Stephanie offered their services when the PMG group met to discuss the matter, and their spacecraft was suitably equipped with the special weapon and flew up to the portal on their way to Mars. They had been provided with maps showing areas where there was no population, so once they were through and were hovering over Mars, they were soon able to select the right spot to drop the bomb.

The whole exercise was carried out with such remarkable speed and efficiency that the Martian force had no time to intercept them before the bomb was dropped with devastating effect, and they were back through the portal on their way back to Earth unscathed. It was a remarkable feat requiring exact timing and speed, and the prime minister was so delighted with the outcome that they were later given bravery honours to mark the occasion.

The effect inside Mars was enormous! Out of the blue, an attack had taken place before anyone could do anything about it. The explosion that followed the attack was gigantic, and the resulting tremors were felt great distances away.

The Chief had been taken entirely by surprise, and there was an uprising demanding that he should be replaced for failing to protect them. Riots took place in the streets as everyone was now afraid of the possibility of another lightning attack taking place at any time without warning. They wanted someone capable of protecting them properly, not to be attacked without warning.

All thoughts of themselves attacking and then populating other planets were suddenly forgotten. What they now wanted was to have proper protection themselves against any further sudden attacks, and by their demonstrations, they made certain that the Chief knew it.

For his part, he knew that unless he could provide this for them, he would be out on his neck, but since he had no idea where the attack had come from, he was soon toppled and replaced in elections.

Travellers returning back to Britain on trading spaceships brought the news that the belligerent Chief of Mars had been replaced. Those in Earth who had carried out the attack saw that, at last, their work had succeeded beyond all expectations, especially when they heard it reported that the new Chief had ordered everyone to concentrate now on protecting their own planet and to forget all about attacking and populating other ones.

It seemed that, at last, the endless threats from Mars had been quelled, and there were joyous celebrations amongst Earth's population, who felt that they could at last get on with their lives without any more fear of the sudden and ominous attacks which had worried them for so many generations.

The planned intention to bring law and order back into Mars had to be thrown into the long grass until they had sorted out their own defence problems, and only then might they be amenable to change, the US president told the UK prime minister, and he agreed when they had another conversation about Mars. But at least, the surprise attack had done the trick!

CHAPTER TWENTY-EIGHT

· · · · · · ●●● ● ●●● · · · · · · ·

Things then started to deteriorate in Jupiter uncontrollably. Their Leader had spent so much of his time concentrating on external threats that he had lost sight of internal politics and justice. More and more money had flown out of the Exchequer for protection purposes that there was very little left for anything else. On top of that, trade in exports from Jupiter to other planets had been severely disrupted by the constant attacks which the trading spaceships had experienced, with their goods and materials being pirated, especially by the Martians.

Their legal system suffered in turn because the judges had their salaries and pensions cut to the bone for economy purposes, leading some of them to accept bribes, and many left the profession altogether for more lucrative occupations.

Naturally, they wanted to keep up their standard of living, and the law was no longer the way to do it. Justice itself suffered as a result because enormous backlogs of cases occurred due to the absence of sufficient judiciary and state aid, so it followed that many of the public's disputes had to go unresolved.

This led to more lawlessness as the wronged took the law into their own hands and employed agencies who were willing to achieve recompense for their clients by using strong arm tactics, kidnappings, and threats of arson of businesses! Not only that, but if you used such an agency, they took up to 40 per cent of the amount recovered, and there was nothing you could do about it!

The Leader now felt completely out of his depth. Everything seemed to be falling down about his ears, much as had happened to the old Chief on Mars, and he didn't know where to turn for help. The trouble was that he seemed to be surrounded by such inept advisers. The little advice he did receive from them was not sensible, in his opinion, and he had nowhere else to turn.

················●··········

It so happened that Yost was on a goodwill trip to Jupiter, arranged long before, and the Leader, hearing about it, asked to see him in desperation, remembering that he was known to have useful connections on Earth.

When he arrived, Yost was installed in the palace and was looked after in style. After his luggage had been delivered to his suite, he put a call through to his old friend Zooba on Earth, telling him that he had arrived safely. He said that he would keep in touch and then went off to have an audience with the Leader.

When he entered the room and approached him, he couldn't believe his eyes. The Leader looked quite haggard and unwell and was clearly under great strain.

When asked about it, the Leader said that they'd ruined their economy, apart from the piracy issue taking its toll, by spending so much of the planet's resources on quelling the Martians' attacks. On top of that, they'd been required to bear part of the expense of developing the new weapon, which itself had nearly crippled them, but that now had, hopefully, brought about the dawn of a new era.

Yost asked how he could help, and the Leader said that if only he could restore law and order, with justice for all, he was convinced that everything would gradually fall back into place satisfactorily. And he wondered if Yost knew of anyone back on Earth who could help him organise it all.

Yost replied that he had a long-standing friend there who had many useful contacts, and he would be happy to have a word with him about it.

The Leader said that he would be very grateful if he would, and they settled down to a meal with the immediate family during which no more was supposed to be said about it. Naturally, however, the same problems kept coming up in conversation, but Yost made no comments on the subject, preferring to wait until he had the opportunity to speak to Zooba about it all.

All he could do in the meantime was to sympathise with the state of things in Jupiter, and he promised them that he would try to think how he could best help them in their predicament.

CHAPTER TWENTY-NINE

·········●·········

As soon as Zooba heard from Yost what was going on in Jupiter, he recalled him back to Earth so that they could consider if there was anyone suitable enough to send out to help the Leader. From what he had heard, he said it would be a mammoth task to turn things around there, and it was most important that the Leader was given the best of help since, one day, Man might well need to go there to live. It would be in their best interests to do what they could to help.

Zooba spoke to the UK prime minister about it whilst Yost was on his way back, after which they both had an audience with the King to obtain his views. His opinions had proved to be of great use to his citizens when times had been hard, and it was not surprising that they turned to him over this.

After very much debate in Parliament, and in the corridors of power, the general consensus was that the Chancellor of the Exchequer should be seconded to Jupiter for, after all, he was the financial expert in that field.

He could take a few civil servants who could stay on after he'd examined all the accounts and sorted out a plan for them to carry through whilst he would then return to his duties here. Earth had sufficient forward planning in place to make the scheme work, and Jupiter would be indebted to it for the help it would receive.

The Chancellor was a man of great integrity and forensic ability. He'd recently pulled around seemingly unsolvable problems in the

United Kingdom, and when he heard that he had been appointed by no less than the King himself, he realised that his reputation must have risen enormously as a consequence.

David, for that was his name, had come from a very poor background in the north of England. He had worked his way diligently through the educational system and had suddenly found himself qualified both as a lawyer and as an accountant, in one of the top jobs in government, controlling the country's finances! It was no wonder, therefore, that he had been selected for this most important task, he thought. Earth's future could depend on his success.

Not only that, but he had previously been called in to give financial and legal advice to other Earth countries and had received several awards for doing so. Going to foreign parts was therefore not in the least daunting for him, although travelling all the way out to Jupiter was going to be in a different class altogether!

He moped around at home, not being sure if he wanted to take on this task on another planet, and so decided to turn to his wife for guidance and support. She was very sensible in his opinion and had always given him useful advice in the past.

She replied by asking him what his gut feeling was, and his reply was that, whilst it sounded strange and dangerous, other humans had been there before and had returned safely. He'd been nominated by the King himself and felt that, however unusual the task, overall he thought it his duty to take it on.

If she was sure that, with him on another planet, she could manage alone, he would go, but if she had any qualms, then he would decline it.

Her main reaction was how brave and yet caring her husband was. She knew how much his work had brought them both such success, and this was, after all, the King wanting his services! She said that she had their children for support whilst he was away, and he shouldn't worry at all about that. She had her own work on the Womens' Guild to occupy her, so he should accept and prepare to go.

Next day, he called his staff together and revealed the situation to them. There were gasps of surprise as they'd all been so immersed in their own compartments of work that this planetary adventure sounded quite fantastic. When it came to being asked who would volunteer to provide backup support and stay on afterwards to see things through, there was at first a silence whilst they thought about it, and then several opted to go with him.

David noticed that the older, more experienced members of his staff were reluctant to go, and these were the very ones he needed. The others were just comparative youngsters looking for excitement and were not likely to be so dedicated to the task and useful to him as they could easily be distracted.

Kenneth was one he particularly wanted to accompany him. He'd been his virtual right-hand man on previous foreign trips, helping out with advice and giving legal-type lectures in other countries suggesting improvements, so he took him aside and asked if he would consider going with him this time. He said how much he would appreciate it if he would agree.

He assured him that he could select as much of the other willing staff as he fancied, so long as he came himself and not to forget that, as the King himself had approved the journey and selected himself, he expected awards would be made on their return and was certain that Kenneth would not be left out.

Kenneth was a man whose wife had unfortunately died young, and living alone, he didn't need to consult anyone, so it didn't take him long to agree to go. David said how pleased he was at his decision, and he was to go off and prepare what they needed to take with. Kenneth, in turn, thanked him for the opportunity which he said sounded most interesting and exciting.

They all gathered at the spaceport and made themselves comfortable for the journey. Yost had said how he would like to go as they might find him useful with dialects or in other ways, and so he became one of the party too.

They had no problem when they reached the exit portal as they each carried return permits which the King himself had organised, and they were soon on their way out into space for the long journey to Jupiter.

In the absence of much conversation, they adopted the custom of telling jokes to each other to while away the time on such interplanetary trips. For some reason, they appreciated senior jokes best. Maybe this was because most of them had old relatives suffering from different disorders, which they found curiously humorous.

This was not funny in itself, of course, but most of the jokes took up extreme situations which were not really likely to happen in real life, and that is where the humour lay. There were deaf people, there were those who couldn't see well, and there were those whose memory was failing.

Yost told them that his kind didn't have any such humour because aliens had developed a way of living full healthy lives until they suddenly dropped dead at a good age. But he was intrigued to hear how humans made humour out of their old people.

David said that they must look into how aliens managed to live long healthy lives in case humans could do the same. He then went on by saying he'd heard a good story only the other day: 'An old man said to his wife that he wished he could still play golf, but his eyesight wasn't good enough any more. His wife suggested he could still play by taking his old friend along as he had good eyesight. So they both turned up at the club, and the old man teed off as he had always done.

'As the ball flew into the distance, he asked his friend if he could see it, and he said, "Of course I can." So they both went down the fairway. Seeing the flag in the distance, the old man asked his old friend where the ball was, and he looked at him sheepishly and replied, "I'm sorry. I'm afraid I've forgotten!"'

They all laughed that one man couldn't remember and the other couldn't see!

Kenneth then chimed in with, 'A man in his sixties agreed to try and fix up his friend from the bowling club with a date, but when the friend was introduced to the woman, he was astonished.

'"She's the ugliest old woman I've ever seen!" he whispered under his breath. "Her hair's falling out, she's hardly got any teeth, she has a wooden leg, and she's only got one eye."

'"I don't know why you're whispering," said the other man. "She's deaf as well!"'

They were all in contortions over that one—how different, they thought, from when aliens grow old.

Yost then gave a version of one he'd heard, 'A middle-aged man was given a course of medicine tablets for two months by his doctor. He asked him if he would be able to play golf.

'"Of course", said the doctor.

'"Oh, that's great", said the man, "because I never could before!"'

They were both amused by that one.

David said they'd better now get ready to land as they were nearing Jupiter, and just as he said it, a violent zooming noise crashed through their ears as a spaceship came very close and opened fire on them. Their pilot took a quick evading action and avoided any damage first time round, but the enemy ship came full circle quickly and attempted to shoot them down again.

David leaned into one of his cases and drew out the miniature new weapon which had recently been developed, and as the spaceship came nearby, he discharged it through a specially designed porthole and scored a direct hit, sending it flying out of control into outer space. As he watched, he could see it disintegrate as it disappeared from sight, and they were all able to breathe a deep sigh of relief.

They asked the pilot if he had any idea where it had come from, and he said that they had recently been experiencing similar attacks and had noticed Orion written on the side of one of them. This meant that those aliens were being as antagonistic as those from Mars had been, and their attacks were becoming particularly disrupting to their timetables, having to delay their journeys to ward them off.

But that aside, the pilot said that the way David had dealt with the attacker was remarkable and wanted to know what weapon he'd used on them. He told him about the new miniaturised weapon and said that when he arrived, he would suggest to the Leader that all their spaceships should be equipped with one.

Meanwhile, he said, he hoped that the recent attacker had found time to report its fate at the hands of a mysterious new weapon before it disappeared and disintegrated. If Orion got the message, all well and good. Otherwise, the use of the weapon itself would make them eventually desist from attacking in the future; he was convinced.

Their eventual landing was uneventful. The control tower staff were so pleased to see them safely down as they'd listened in to the whole frightening episode as it had unfolded.

The party was whisked off to the palace where they were to stay, and the nine of them were spread out in interconnecting rooms. This was suitable to enable them to consult together, but they lost a certain amount of privacy in their off times by the arrangement.

After a good night's sleep, David said that he didn't like the arrangement, and instead, he arranged for Kenneth and his secretary to share one suite, leaving himself alone at last, which he found much more convenient. The others made do as best they could.

Kenneth, being a single man, had struck up a friendship with Helen, who had become his secretary back in London, so they were quite happy sharing a suite together. She found him to be very personable and thoughtful and therefore had no qualms when asked to join the group to be his secretary.

Although they tried to keep their relationship on a professional basis, things seemed different for her once they'd arrived, being so distant from her homeland, and she was particularly conscious of being so far away from Earth. Although becoming more common, travelling such very long distances didn't suit all the humans who tried it, and she was no exception.

It made her particularly vulnerable as she could find no normality except in Kenneth's company, and as a result, they grew closer and closer together.

David had spotted this and spoke to Kenneth about it, but he pleaded with him not to change the present arrangement as, at least, it gave her a little security whilst with someone she knew, and David agreed that it made sense to keep things as they were.

By now, the word had gone round that a group had arrived from Earth to change things, and there were those, like the strong-armed characters dispensing their own form of justice, who were not at all happy with this development.

They were doing so well out of their 40 per cent of recoveries of debts that they were naturally loath to see the court systems operating properly again and decided to do something about it.

They knew, of course, that the group was staying in the palace and that gaining access was not going to be easy. So they decided to adopt a disguise. Four of them waylaid a van on its way with daily fresh provisions for the palace. Having tied up the van's occupants, two of them donned the outfits of the driver and his mate whilst the other two hid in the back.

Fortunately for them, the guard at the gate knew the van was due because it was its time to do so, and he automatically opened the gate to let them in. It was still dark, but he could just make out the usual uniforms sitting on the front seats, and so nothing untoward occurred to him.

They drove round to the kitchen door and rushed in, wielding guns and knives, only to find one doorkeeper on duty as it was still too early for the rest of the staff to have arrived. He was horrified as they tied him up and told him not to make any noise. At least they weren't going to kill him, he consoled himself!

Getting in was one thing, but finding where the humans were was another. They hid themselves in a storeroom and took the doorman with them. Once the staff had arrived and had made up the various breakfasts, it should be possible, they calculated, to follow them to the rooms, although how to distinguish between the normal residents' and the humans' rooms remained a problem.

The plan was to frighten the humans just enough to make them flee back to Earth. Anything worse, and they knew that the security services would be sure to hunt them down and incarcerate them for many years, if not to execute them.

The four of them then crept up the stairs to the first floor, managing not to be seen, and waited behind some screens. It was obvious that this floor had their victims staying in it because the suites had names on their doors and clearly contained the bedrooms.

As the food came up, carried by three waiters, the four heard them point out which room got which tray, and this enabled them to distinguish between the humans' rooms and the others' by the type of food brought. The Leader had provided for the humans to have their own kind of food so far as was possible, so their rooms were soon identified that way.

As soon as the waiters had left, the four broke into one room after another until they found them and had brandished their weapons at the humans, warning them that they were not welcome there and had better return to Earth if they knew what was good for them. They were extremely menacing and clearly meant what they said.

They left as quickly as they'd arrived and managed to get out back through the kitchens and away in the van before anyone had the resourcefulness to raise the alarm; they were so shocked.

David and Kenneth realised that they needed better protection. The ladies had been frightened out of their skins, and a repeat of the episode would certainly cause them psychological damage.

They enquired where the Leader's room was and went along to see him. As they arrived, he had just heard what had happened to his guests and couldn't apologise enough. He immediately ordered security to be put on full alert and ordered a chase to be arranged to bring the offenders to justice.

It turned out that someone had reported the van rushing off at high speed. It had just missed him because he managed to jump out of its path, but he was able to take down and then report its number plate to the police, which had enabled them to be spotted and put under arrest, awaiting being charged.

The case was given full priority on the Leader's orders, and a line-up soon revealed that these were the same as had broken in and threatened the humans, so the court had no hesitation in sending them down for several years. In passing sentence, the judge said that he hoped that their colleagues took note of this penalty, and that, indeed, if there were any more such occurrences, the sentences would be much more severe.

CHAPTER THIRTY

· · · · · ●●●●● ● ●●●●● · · · · ·

A messenger came to their rooms, and David and Kenneth were asked to attend a summit meeting and to bring their staff with them, and the Leader had his top advisers with him there.

The Leader opened the proceedings by introducing his advisers and then turned immediately to the recent attack, apologising again for having allowed it to happen in his own palace. He said that he had arranged for the full trial to be printed and broadcasted as a warning to others and that he understood that everyone was much more security conscious as a result.

David said that he reckoned that by dispensing justice on the attackers so efficiently, it would stand as a good warning for others not to try the same.

The Leader said that the main purpose of the meeting was to tackle the overwhelming problem of disorder in his planet. It was lucky that a passer-by had, by chance, been able to record the number plate which had brought the attackers to justice, but this wasn't the normal situation where the crooks were now getting away with their crimes most of the time.

David responded and said, 'I have given a great deal of thought to your problem, Leader, and I think that I have the solution. You remember we know about the nearby uninhabited planet and had thought to occupy it if your or our planets became uninhabitable? Well, I suggest that you should pass a new law which will allow your judges to have an additional penalty available, and that is to be able to order deportation to that planet!

'When they arrive, they can gradually build up a colony, and eventually, when they have served their sentence, they can be considered for return here if they were thought to have been rehabilitated sufficiently.

'The very thought of deportation, especially to another undeveloped planet, ought to bring fear to the hearts of anyone thinking of breaking the law, and I reckon that law and order will soon be restored through fear of such a fate.

'Of course, some basic installations will have to be constructed there to accommodate the prisoners, but I'm sure that just by passing the deportation law, the whole population will be scared witless of committing any offence, and very few individuals will actually have to be deported. What do you think of the idea?'

'I think that's a novel and quite remarkable solution,' the Leader said. 'If that won't bring the criminal fraternity into line and make them go out and get regular work for themselves, I don't know what will.'

David said, 'I'm glad my idea appeals to you. Also, we have been installing robot judges on Earth which are proving quite a success, and maybe, you would like to adopt this idea as well. This frees you from judges who have become so self-important that they tend to think themselves superior beings and entitled to great rewards and riches and who, I understand, have gone on strike for more reward more than once recently.

'Apart from regularly programming these judgebots, as they are known, with the latest laws and decisions for them to follow, there is very little expense involved, and the saving will be immense. It has worked well on Earth, and I cannot see why it shouldn't here.'

'Yes, you are quite right. Our judges have been holding up the whole judicial system with all sorts of repercussions, as you can imagine,' the Leader replied. 'Maybe we could introduce your—what did you call them?—judgebots gradually, not to upset the judges too much.'

'I'm afraid that won't do,' David said. 'We have to take bold decisions if we are to re-establish law and order, and allowing the judges to dictate any part of the reforms is asking for disaster!'

'Yes, I see your point,' the Leader said. 'Then that is what we'll do. As soon as the judgebots are up and running, we can retire the judges on full pension to keep them quiet.'

David said that they would have to see what was available when the time came. He needed to see the state accounts before he could advise on that, but he really thought that it would probably be on half pension only until things got sorted out generally. He added that as he understood that the Leader's people lived to a ripe old age in good health, it was quite likely that in retirement from the bench, the judges could well take up other occupations such as lecturing on the law or indeed representing litigants in court, which would tide them over if they were first put on half pension.

The Leader commended David on his sensible analysis of the situation and said that he would follow his advice. He wondered afterwards why he had not thought of it himself but then recalled that was why he had wanted the help of a human brain in the first place— and such an experienced one at that.

David was just about to explain how useful it would be to install a protective veil around Jupiter when there was an enormous crashing sound out in the grounds. They all rushed to the window and could see that an unusually large spaceship had landed very awkwardly and was lying at an angle in a hole.

The Leader summoned his elite troops to go and investigate. They approached the ship gingerly in case it might explode or, alternatively, attack them with its weapons. This was a very unusual occurrence because these ships normally had inbuilt guidance systems to prevent bad landings, and something must have gone wrong with its electronics.

As they watched from the window, they saw an exit door open up, and down walked none other than the Chief from Mars! He was instantly recognised by the captain of the troops, and he went forward to help him negotiate the awkward angle the ship had landed at.

He saluted the Chief, who told him that he had been travelling past Jupiter when their controls went haywire and had brought them down next to the Leader's palace, of all places!

The captain didn't think it right for him to reveal the presence of the electronic installations they'd put in around the palace which firstly took over the controls of any unannounced or unexpected spaceships flying in the vicinity and then brought them down for investigation. So he simply said that he was pleased that they had landed in one piece and asked if he would like him to accompany him inside the palace, possibly to talk to his Leader.

The Chief was in two minds about this but realised that he found himself in a precarious situation on foreign soil with only a handful of technicians on board as backup and had very little choice in the matter.

A message was sent up to the Leader, telling him who had arrived and asking if he wanted to see him or to just lock him up.

When David heard who had arrived, he advised that this could be a golden opportunity for the two leaders and himself to iron out their long-standing differences and suggested that the Chief should be brought in to the Leader's presence for discussions.

His spaceship had to be immobilised, of course, just in case its technicians found a way of overriding the electronics which had brought it down, and that was seen to first.

The Chief was then led by the captain up to where the others were, and the Leader said how unfortunate it was that the Chief's journey had been disrupted as he sat him down in front of him.

He was quite shocked from the sudden landing but gradually pulled himself together in order to talk sensibly to his arch-enemy.

When asked how his spaceship had been forced down, the Chief was told that Jupiter's scientists had developed the system some time back and that it had proved to be an excellent defence weapon, completely disorienting spaceships as they were brought down.

Its design involved using magmatite which they'd found under the sea at Bermuda when they'd happened upon the place. This had been found to have been the cause of many ships and aircraft disappearing without trace in what became known as the Bermuda Triangle as it had caused them to become disoriented and run out of fuel. The magmatite is a mixture of volcanic rock and sand, which has strong magnetic properties which deviated compasses as planes flew over it and caused ships to sink because it lay unobserved just beneath the ocean's surface and tore open their lower parts through its remarkable strength.

'The wreckage of ships and planes descended into the depths of the sea, never to be found again because man could never go down that deep to find them, and the area also became known as the Devil's Triangle,' he said.

'So it was ordered that quantities were collected and incorporated into our armaments for use in the same way,' he concluded.

Indeed, he went on, they had developed a miniaturised weapon as well which, although small and transportable, was so powerful that it had actually destroyed an attacking spaceship recently. The Leader wanted to make the best impression on the Chief whilst he had this chance, with him in front of him, to make sure that he would realise that if Mars ever tried to attack Jupiter again, Mars would certainly be on the losing side.

So far as the Leader was concerned, he had got his message across well because he could see the Chief's reaction. There was nothing more to waste his time on. He had other urgent matters to attend to. The Chief would be allowed to return unharmed so he could carry this message back to his people.

The Chief withdrew, accompanied by an officer, and was allowed to return to his spaceship. He climbed awkwardly up the ramp because of the angle at which it had landed and ordered the door to be shut behind him.

The ship was powered up with its secret secondary motors which had not been disabled after he had landed. At the very moment it began taking off, the Chief, in his fury, ordered shells to be discharged directly at the palace!

The ship was capable of very high speeds, even more than most spaceships, and it had disappeared from sight long before the palace staff had time to realise what had happened.

Fortunately, just after the Chief had left the room, the Leader had gone off in his flycar to an official engagement elsewhere, so he missed the ensuing blast. But when he received the message about the attack, he cancelled the engagement on the grounds of national security and returned to see what was needed.

He was furious with the Mars Chief for having done this and also with himself for having allowed him to go back unheeded. There was clearly no way that he could treat him decently in the future, and he resolved to take every opportunity to settle the score.

David and Kenneth were unharmed in the attack as their rooms were at the back, but they and their staff were certainly shocked by the whole episode. They decided that the best thing they could do would be to get on with their tasks, and so they gathered in David's suite to make further plans. The quicker they got done and out of there back to Earth, the better, they all thought, if this was the sort of thing that could happen!

· · · · · · · · · ● · · · · · · · · · · ·

The shells had left a gaping hole in the palace wall, and the criminal gangs opposing change soon got to hear of it. Here was another chance, they thought, to get in and frighten off the humans once and for all. Two groups with the same object combined together, each one charged with taking on the humans separately.

They both managed to steal inside, dressed as workmen, before the real contractors got there to repair the damage, and they spread out quietly through the building, looking for the right rooms. No one suspected them, as workmen were expected to be about to assess the damage anyway, so they were able to move about freely.

The Leader realised that there was now a serious security risk to the palace until it was repaired, and so he decided that his family should adjourn to his summer palace on a lakeside setting not too far away. He told the human group that it would be best if they all joined him there. It didn't take them long to gather up the few belongings they'd brought from Earth and were out of a back door and into a helicopter on their way before those searching for them could find them.

They went into different rooms in the palace, looking for the humans, only to find every one of them deserted! Getting themselves out of the palace was going to be another matter. It was all very well being dressed up as contractors, but the staff soon began to wonder if they were genuine. Indeed, as soon as the real ones came on-site, they soon identified the false ones, who were then put under arrest until the Leader decided what to do with them.

Meanwhile, as soon as the Chief had taken off back towards Mars, it so happened that one of David's colleagues, who had gone to the spaceport to try out one of the latest space fighter planes at the suggestion of the Leader, was in the air in one of them, experiencing the exhilarating speed which it was capable of achieving.

The pilot suddenly spotted the Chief's well-known spacecraft going in the same direction and reported in what he had seen. The news was immediately passed on to the Leader, and as he was so furious with him for the damage he'd caused, the space fighter was ordered to give chase and, if given the chance, to destroy it.

The pilot carried out his orders, whilst David's man looked on in horror as he'd overheard what was about to happen. They gradually caught up with the Chief's craft and, using the new weapon, shot it out of the air to its destruction.

The Leader was told the news immediately. He realised that another chief would soon be appointed and only hoped that he would be less hostile than the last one.

Having destroyed the old Chief, he couldn't help feeling a pang of regret as he'd known him for so long and was used to having him as his arch-enemy. But he would soon get over it, he told himself.

CHAPTER THIRTY-ONE

••••••••●•••••••

The Leader's summer palace was set in very lush grounds beside one of the most beautiful lakes in the country, and the whole estate was immaculately maintained by a group of gardeners who had been there for many years.

One or two of them still remembered the previous Leaders and their particular requirements, especially the ones who had arranged to import some rare trees from other planets to adorn their palaces' grounds.

The children of the gardeners, or some of them, traditionally took over when their parents died off. Being on Jupiter, their parents' good health, short of an accident, normally allowed them to work until they died, so their children sometimes grew to a senior age before being able to take over. And in some cases, they couldn't help being frustrated by having to wait for their turn.

Some of them, wanting to get on, tended secretly to resent this. A couple of them were getting on in age and felt that it was time that they were better rewarded than the seniors were since they were actually doing most of the heavy work. In their frustration, their thoughts turned to the Leader who had the most rewarding job of all. Maybe he could right this wrong.

They'd been told that he was coming with his family and with some humans, so chatting together during a break, they thought up the idea of disguising themselves as indoor staff and confronting him with their demands. It was an outlandish idea and fraught with danger, but they thought it worth the risks involved.

The Leader had realised, following the attack on his palace, that security needed tightening up even further, so he had given orders that his summer palace should have its security enhanced, especially during the times he and his family were in residence.

The head of security there was in a dilemma. He was suddenly expected to provide extra security without any notice. How was he to interview applicants and check on any criminal records in a hurry?

He talked it over with his aide who suggested that the best source of additional security would be from those already vetted and employed there. The obvious pool of such appointments was from the gardeners, he said, because he was sure that the gardens wouldn't suffer if some of the gardeners were employed as extra security staff. After all, as soon as the Leader returned to the city, they could stand down and return to their gardening.

The head of security thought this was an excellent plan and asked his aide to see which gardeners would like to take up the posts of additional security.

As soon as the young rebellious gardeners got to hear of this, they put themselves forward. Here was an ideal opportunity to get access to the indoors and the chance to approach the Leader. *Who would suspect familiar faces standing in during the Leader's time in residence?* they thought.

Once appointed, however, they were more than surprised to be put on outside perimeter duty instead and not inside at all! It was thought that, being gardeners, they would know their way around the grounds far better than anyone else, which is why their duties were to be outside.

They were furious with this outcome. Their only consolation was that they were paid better as security staff than as mere gardeners! Otherwise, they were back where they started unless, of course, they could stay on as security staff afterwards somehow.

· · · · · · · · ● ● · · · · · · · · · · ·

The Leader meanwhile called everyone together again in the main dining room and, over a lunchtime meal, set out his plans for Jupiter's future.

He opened by saying, 'There will always be room here for human beings to settle if Earth eventually becomes uninhabitable. Indeed, we find them to be a pleasant and experienced people who can teach us useful new ways in technological and AI methodology, and it is decided that if any of them wish to settle here right now, they will be more than welcome to do so.

'So far as law and order are concerned, we have decided to adopt the judgebot idea, giving it a trial run in sample courts. And if it proves to be as successful as I expect it to be, we can then retire our judges who will then be free to take up other legal work if they wish, to supplement the generous pensions I propose awarding them.

'We will never ignore our defence responsibilities, however, and I do hope that the new Chief on Mars will prove to be much more amicable, and less hostile, than the last one so that we can look forward to the time when we can spend less on defence and more on our citizens' prosperity.'

He then invited David to say a few words on behalf of the humans, so David replied, 'I must say how we all appreciate your hospitality and your assurance of a safe haven for us if we ever need it. It is a great consolation to know that a safe harbour always awaits us, and I will certainly consult with my colleagues as to who wishes to stay on.

'During our pleasant stay here, we have found many similarities between our two planets, and the devices for breathing and so on have proved most effective. The simple idea, for example, of adapting our shoes with magnets to counter the lack of the gravity pull which we are used to has made walking about so much simpler for us.

'Whenever we have walked through your streets, we have been welcomed with smiles, and we have always found your people to be most helpful.

'As to the courts systems, I suggest that there is room for robots to take over routine legal tasks as well, which will free up the existing staff for more productive work. There might well be other sectors of your economy where robotics can play their part, and I can get some of my people back on Earth to see what scope there is for this to be done here.

'With your permission, Leader, I suggest that we should establish a commission to look into all these possibilities from Jupiter's point of view so that, by combining the two efforts here and on Earth, we can maximise as much economies as possible for you.'

The Leader was very impressed with David's ideas and the far-seeing economies he clearly had in mind, so he said that he welcomed his ideas wholeheartedly and that they should get on with their plans as quickly as possible. 'The economy needed a boost, and the quicker it got it, the better,' he said.

The Leader asked David to stay behind when the lunch meeting had finished, and they sat together in a small anteroom at the back to discuss further details of the plans.

It was just as well that they'd left the dining room when they did because, straight after they'd gone into the anteroom and sat down to talk, there was an almighty explosion, and the front end of the dining room had completely disappeared!

A rocket had been fired at the summer palace, and it had destroyed the whole front section, together with any unfortunate staff who had happened to be there clearing up. It had come out of the blue and was like a Second World War V2 rocket from the previous century, which always struck without warning.

The palace radar system had picked up a signal from its motors, but it was too late to do anything about it. Engineers were sent in once the rubble had settled to try to identify anything about it which would point to where it had come from.

One of them came across a small piece of shrapnel which bore the name Orion, and this was immediately reported to the Leader whose first thought was that the only alternatives were that it had been discharged either on purpose or by mistake. The latter theory didn't seem feasible, so regretfully, he had no choice other than to arrange for a reprisal attack on that planet.

Just as he'd made that decision, however, another piece was found bearing the name Mars in bold lettering, so it was obvious, after all, that Orion had sold parts of the rocket to Mars who had then made up the whole weapon. It was a Martian rocket after all!

What a horrible coincidence that both of his palaces had been attacked within a short time of each other, he thought. If this was going to become the norm, he was going to have to build down underground to be sure of his family's safety or, somehow, destroy all these attackers at source.

What the Leader didn't know at that stage was that the whole rocket had in fact been imported from Orion by Mars and that it hadn't been discharged by Orion at all! It was only when yet another piece of shrapnel was found bearing the name of a Martian company that he realised that the new Martian Chief was as hostile as the previous one had been!

He sent a message to the Chief that he held him personally responsible for the damage he had caused and was taking the matter to the Interplanetary Court of Justice (as it had now become) for adjudication. Mars had signed up to that court's jurisdiction, and he expected Mars to be represented there at the forthcoming hearing, he told him.

The Chief was in a quandary. Maybe the evidence was insufficient for the court to find against him anyway, and he would be cleared. On the other hand, he knew that the penalties for such an unprovoked attack were likely to be substantial. Could he take the chance and not turn up at the trial? He didn't know, of course, that the markings on the shrapnel were to be given in evidence and would provide convincing evidence against him.

The day of the trial arrived, and everyone took their place as the three judges took their seats. Looking across at the defendant's side, the Chief Justice asked where the defendant was, but nobody could say.

The attorney for the complainant said that he'd had no communication from the defendant's side and had no idea if he was coming or even if he was represented.

The three judges put their heads together and announced that the trial would proceed in the defendant's absence. If he turned up, he could of course intervene, but the court's time was not to be wasted, and they asked the complainant's lawyer to begin and open the case for hearing.

He went through the events of the rocket attack which was clearly contrary to planetary law. Details of the damage were enumerated, and the judges took notes. Exhibits were brought in at the judges' request showing the incriminating markings, and at that very moment, in walked the Martian Chief himself, and he took his place at the front bench.

When asked to account for his failure to attend on time and if he was represented, he explained that his flight had been delayed by marauding spacecraft which, he said, were clearly marked as being from Jupiter. When asked if he had any corroborating evidence of this, he said that it was naturally impossible to produce any. As for representation, he had decided none was necessary. He was innocent.

The exhibits were shown to him, one by one, and he was cross-examined as to why the markings were clearly shown to incriminate his planet in the attack.

At first taken aback by this evidence but trying not to show it, he told the court, 'Unfortunately, Your Worships, we have in our planet certain rebellious elements who want nothing more than to upset the order of things. Some of them have formed a gang which has got hold of a couple of our space fighters, and they have been roaming the galaxy, causing mayhem and leaving behind them, probably unintentionally, traces such as these exhibits, leading back to incriminating the Mars planet.

'None of this has been done with my authority, and I regret that damage has been done to Jupiter's palaces.'

'How do you know that Jupiter's palaces were attacked?' the complainant's attorney demanded, thinking that he had undermined the Chief's pretence of innocence. 'You were not actually in court when this was given in evidence, were you?'

Thinking quickly on his feet, the Chief replied that he'd had a report that this had happened and had reprimanded those involved, stripping them of their rank and imprisoning them.

'Well, where did that report come from, and who sent it?' demanded Jupiter's lawyer.

'In my position as Chief, I receive all sorts of reports daily, and I'm afraid that I have no recollection,' replied the Chief.

Jupiter's lawyer could see that whatever was thrown at him, the Chief was crafty enough to be able to come up with a plausible answer each time. He closed his case by asking the court to find in Jupiter's favour, and they adjourned to deliberate.

When they resumed, the Chief Justice said, 'This has been a very difficult case to decide. We have been given contradicting evidence of the events which took place, and even the exhibits we've been shown have been explained away by evidence about these rogue pilots, whom we have been told suddenly appear from nowhere.

'It seems to us that we cannot justify our casting doubt on the veracity of the evidence given on oath by the Martian Chief himself. We have no reason to doubt his word and accordingly, in law, hereby exonerate him from any personal culpability.

'However, we are mindful of the damage caused to the complainant's property, and on his own admission, the defendant has confirmed in evidence that the rogue pilots he refers to are from his planet. Accordingly, we find in favour of the complainant on this aspect of the matter, and the defendant is ordered to provide sufficient resources to the complainant to repair the damage caused.

'The court will now appoint an assessor who will travel to Jupiter, at the defendant's expense, and he or she will assess the damage and supervise the repairs on the court's behalf. However, if we receive any report of obstruction to this court's order, the defendant will be held personally responsible.'

Looking across to the Martian Chief, the Chief Justice made it clear by his manner and beady eye that he would stand no nonsense from him and expected him to obey the court's decision.

It only remained for the court to award the full costs of the hearing against Mars and added that they expected that all rogue pilots would immediately be brought under control on Mars to prevent any similar incursions.

The Chief was then asked what guarantees he could give the court that the damages and costs would be paid. He was told that until the court could be sure of this, he would be detained in open prison until a substantial deposit against these expenses had been paid into court. It was not that they didn't trust him, he said, but the court had to ensure that justice was done and the works properly funded.

Not having any security for costs with him, the Chief was unable to provide the guarantee the court required, and he was carted off. He was put under strict guard but given an intergalactic transponder to arrange for the deposit.

He put an urgent call through to his chancellor to arrange for these substantial costs to be sent in but was stunned to find his request queried. Why, he was asked, had he defended the case instead of just paying for the damage? There would have been virtually no costs to pay, and they wouldn't have had to pay for the court assessor to come over, with all the additional expense which that incurred. It had turned out to be a complete waste of money, and he would be expected to foot at least part of the total bill personally, he was told!

He was quite shocked, to say the least. If the exchequer refused to pay, he could be incarcerated there for the rest of his life!

Imprisonment, even in an open prison, was certainly not an option, so he sent a message back to his bank to transfer sufficient from his deposit account into his current account and then to send it directly to the court, making sure, of course, that it was marked as being in respect of his case.

It hurt him considerably that his savings had been so depleted, but at least, he would now be freed, and he could get reimbursed, at least partially, when he got back.

Somehow, the bank clerk confused three of the digits he gave her, probably because of solar storms wavering the sound between the planets during his giving instructions, so as is normal in these cases, the money was placed in the bank's reserve account until it could be found its intended home.

The Chief sat there waiting day after day, and still, he was not released, so he made further enquiries at his bank and was relieved to find that they had eventually realised the error and that the money had finally reached the court just under a week later.

At last, the guards came in and said he was free to go but that the assessor would be accompanying him. They became quite friendly on the journey back, mostly because of the Chief's effort to put him at his ease, hoping this way somehow to get the final rebuilding costs reduced.

When they'd landed, the assessor was put up at their top luxury hotel. This would not have been the Chief's first choice because of the expense involved, but the court had booked the suite directly in the Chief's name in advance, so there was nothing he could do about it.

As soon as he reached the city palace, the Chief gave orders for the rogue fighters to be chased down much more rigorously. He didn't want any more experiences such as he had just gone through, and he certainly couldn't face prison again, even an open one.

The court's assessor began work on the project and, on examining one of the rooms normally used for display purposes, found certain damaged artefacts. Far from being helpful, the assessor found a number of items there and in other rooms which he insisted should be included in the official inventory of works. The most costly ones related to certain very old frescoes which had formed part of the original decorative finish and which he insisted should be restored.

The Chief tried his best to prevent this and said that these had long ago deteriorated and had not been thought worth renovating, but the assessor insisted on them being done, thus increasing the expected total cost even further.

The Chief's aide queried whether any of these costs could be claimed for on their insurance, but when they enquired, it was soon pointed out by the insurers, to the Chief's dismay, that there was an exclusion on the policy for attacks of that nature, as they clearly constituted acts of war.

CHAPTER THIRTY-TWO

· · · · · · ●● ● ●● · · · · · · ·

David and Kenneth were mulling over all these events with their staff. The Interplanetary Court of Justice certainly seemed finally to have been very effective as between planets, but internally, within each planet, there still seemed to be endless causes of dissension.

'Generally, these appeared to stem from failing economies caused by trade wars between the planets, which led to the populace suffering hardships from unusually heavy tariffs, which ought not be happening,' David said.

He said that he had come to realise that unless this Gordian knot could be cut, delicate and important relationships could easily relapse beyond recall, and all the plans for going to live in each others' planets, if the worst came to the worst, would be dashed forever, leaving everyone nowhere to find sanctuary. And all human and alien life would eventually disappear forever, just as though the so-called Big Bang hadn't occurred!

Kenneth said that this certainly mustn't be allowed to happen, and he proposed that several planets, including Earth and Enceladus, should send representatives to a grand meeting in order to thrash out these ridiculous petty local arguments, which had grown out of all proportion, and to bring back law and order so that life could continue to exist.

But who was capable of arranging it? The humans obviously couldn't do so on their own, but in conjunction with the Leader of Jupiter, he and David thought that it could be made possible and that it could just about be achieved.

The Interplanetary Court was formally asked to intervene by the Leader, and a hearing was scheduled for everyone involved to send a representative along to have their say. The court had been given jurisdiction in many fields when it had been established, and such a dispute over trade, having such serious repercussions, was ideal for it to adjudicate upon.

Indeed the Court had also been given legislative powers and was able to correct any deficiencies or loopholes in the law on its own volition, and immediately, it discovered them.

Every leader sent a representative along lest they miss out on what was decided. They were all heard in turn, and it appeared to the court, at the end of the giving of evidence, that by simply balancing one tariff against another, they quite often cancelled each other out.

The Court ordered that it was clear that all tariffs should be abandoned, making trade far less expensive all round, and this left more resources within the individual economies for every member of the populace to enjoy. This, in turn, led to far less internal strife, and normal trade was resumed.

The planets' political systems now no longer depended on each party blaming the other for their citizens' poverty, but at last, it became possible to find time to attempt to resolve important matters such as global warming and finally bringing about the ending of inter-galactic warfare.

Of course, there were local arguments which were now able to be resolved by the judgebots in the area courts. They had proved to be a success because personal inhibitions or psychological hang-ups no longer took any part in court judgements. They were simple robots who could not be corrupted or threatened.

The judgebots took no account of anything other than the cross-examined facts and made their determinations accordingly, just as they had been programmed to do. Constantly updated on the latest laws, they passed their judgements without fear or favour.

David and Kenneth felt that by having referred everything to the Interplanetary Court of Justice and installed the judgebots, they had achieved what they had set out to do, so David put a call through to the UK prime minister and told him what had occurred and how successful he thought their visit had been.

He couldn't have been more shocked with the reply, to say the least! Apparently, whilst they had been away, there had been an attack on London and that, unfortunately, there had been many casualties as a result. When asked who was responsible for it, the prime minister said that he believed, from reports he had received, that it had come from a far-distant planet which had not been involved in the main court settlement between planets.

Somehow, it seemed, a solitary space fighter had broken through or had bribed its way through the veil's portal and had chosen London as its target. After it had discharged its shells, it had been brought down electronically and was immediately shrouded over so that it could not depart again, and they were just about to investigate further, he said, and hopefully would be able to interrogate the occupants.

David and Kenneth were recalled to Earth with their immediate staff. Any juniors who felt that they could make their homes in Jupiter were allowed to stay. There would be plenty of work for them, given their specialised experience.

Unfortunately for the occupants of the space fighter, they had not expected to have to cope with the different atmospheric pressures found on Earth, and they were unable to come out of their craft because of this. Their backup motor had also been immobilised electronically, so they just had to sit inside whilst their fate was decided.

Without their knowledge, the temporary cover was suddenly removed, and at the same time, the whole spaceship was hauled aloft by a crane which had been brought on-site, and it was taken to the nearest lock-up hangar for closer examination. They were shocked by being raised up like that since, for all they knew, they might be dropped in water and drowned.

The UK prime minister thought it best to call upon the services of Yost, and he asked Zooba to find him and bring him there. Being from a strange distant galaxy, the occupants of the craft might well not speak the English language, he said, but Yost might find a way of being able to communicate with them.

He could, of course, have had them destroyed there and then, but it occurred to him that they might know something useful which he, or the closer galactic community, could use.

If it was right, he thought, that they had come from a distant planet, there could well be things that they could tell which could usefully add to their little existing knowledge of the far galaxies and prove useful for their own protection in the long run.

David and Kenneth's party arrived back in London about the same time as Yost got there, and they met up, by arrangement, at the BT Tower headquarters of the prime minister's PMG group.

The main decision arising from their discussions was that Yost should first go and try to communicate with the occupants of the craft, so he went along to the hangar whilst the others observed from a distance.

It wasn't until he'd gone through trying different languages through a portal that he hit upon the right one and was finally able to communicate with them, although not entirely.

They told him that they were very frightened by their predicament, and he tried to put them at their ease, but until they had more information, they said that they couldn't help trembling all over from the shock of the unexpected events and from finding themselves unable to escape from this very strange environment.

It turned out that the information they were able to impart was far more useful than had been expected. Yost had persuaded them into believing that their lives depended on their cooperation, and they were able to reveal information which was quite stunning and remarkable.

It seemed that preparations were being made back in their planet for a major attack on many of the other planets, including Earth, and their own craft had been sent to carry out a preliminary reconnaissance over the British Isles to find a suitable base where they could establish their central control. Others had been sent to other planets for the same purpose.

They also revealed that their own planet had become heavily overcrowded and could no longer sustain its population, which was why their Head Commander, as he was called, had decided on this course of action. His intention was, they said, that if they could subdue every viable planet, they would have all the options for survival open to them by inhabiting one after the other as necessary, for many centuries to come, whatever might befall them by way of any natural catastrophes.

Yost said that he could understand such a plan but told them that it wasn't right to involve every planet like that and that, in any case, it would cause an almighty galactic war. He secretly thought to himself that it was just as well that they now had prior warning so they could prepare for what now appeared to be the final galactic attack which, if successful, would wipe out all extraterrestrials, and even Earth itself.

The first thing he did on instructions was to order the captain of the ship to relay to the Head Commander the fact that hitherto secret magnetic forces, which were only to be found in Earth's waters, had brought his craft down and that they were prisoners. He was also to say that this secret had been shared with friendly Jupiter and other planets and, because the device had been supplied to the others, that any such attack would prove to be ill-considered and would be very costly.

In reply, the Head Commander said that he blamed the captain for having lost control of his craft and that he didn't believe the story of this ridiculous magnetic force. His fate was now in his own hands, he told him, and he had no intention of sending anyone to risk trying to save him.

When Yost translated this message into English, the UK prime minister passed the information on to the US president, asking for his suggestions how to deal with the matter. The response he received surprised him. His proposal was that they should demonstrate, through US's newly invented visual transponder exactly what had befallen the stricken craft by replicating the whole event for the Commander to observe it for himself. If that didn't put him off attacking, he didn't know what would.

Yost was instructed to inform the Commander that a visual demonstration would be transmitted within the hour and that this would convince him of the truth of the matter.

Everything was put in place ready for the demonstration, and a message was sent to the Commander, who said that he was ready to watch. A spaceplane was photographed flying in the air, and the Commander was shown its controls to confirm that nothing was being done by the pilot to bring the craft down. The Commander was asked to give the order for the craft to be brought down, and the magnet device was operated, and down it came, even making a controlled smooth landing this time.

The demonstration was very effective, and although the Commander wondered if the plane's controls had been operated remotely somehow to bring it down without any magnetism, he decided that he really had to be sensible over it. The demonstration certainly convinced him, he told Yost, and he was immediately ordering the recall of all his forces and would be happy to attend a peace conference in the near future. If during that period he could find out the truth about the magnetic device, one way or the other, he would then know for certain.

However, in the meantime, he had no intention of recalling anyone. He couldn't bring himself to trust what he'd just seen and wasn't really convinced by the demonstration he'd watched. In any case, he thought, his own crafts were likely to be much more sophisticated than the one used in the demonstration. Indeed, he thought further and decided to equip his forces with anti-magnetic equipment, now that he knew how the single craft had been disabled.

He instructed his scientists to invent the necessary equipment only to find that they soon came back, telling him that it was impossible to devise anything effective from what was available on their planet.

They told him that any antidote to the magnetic equipment could only be found on Earth so far as they knew, so he was right back where he started, looking for a countermeasure which would be effective to provide protection for his forces! And to get hold of it, he had to get it from Earth!

Somehow, he would have to install an undercover spy in London to try to get enough information about this magnetite and to tap the British scientists' knowledge as to what they thought might override its magnetic force. *Sooner said than done*, he thought to himself. And in any case, it would probably have to be manufactured on Earth because of the different conditions where his own engineers lived.

What if there was no countermeasure anyway? His forces would be helpless as soon as they approached any planet that had it, and there was no knowing which ones had been supplied with the magnetite anyway.

He conjectured whether some sort of casing could be developed which could repel the magnetic force of the magnetite, similar to the ones used on the early space capsules when they returned into Earth's atmosphere, but once again, his scientists said that what was necessary for even that was unavailable there.

In the end, he had to admit defeat without a battle! But it was not in his nature to do so. His tenure in office could well be on the line if he failed to produce what he had led his citizens to expect of him when he was elected. He'd promised them their safety even if their planet had imploded.

Maybe, on second thought, it was still worth trying to infiltrate the laboratories on Earth. A disguise as a human would be necessary, and as they had already developed a way of replicating one, that would not be a problem. It seemed to him that they were good at some things but not at others.

What worried him, however, was what secrets the crew of the stricken craft were revealing to those on Earth. How much did they know of his full intentions, for example? Could they undermine his new plans by revealing something they'd overheard?

He couldn't even be sure that they hadn't listened in to his internal communications and passed them on to the Earthlings in order to save their necks whilst they were encased in their disabled craft!

He concluded that his own future lay in the hands of others now, the very thought of which he hated. And unless he was able to be sensible enough to put his emotions to one side and calmly calculate the best way forward, he could well see himself thrown out of office in a very short time and out in the cold.

............●............

Back on the ground, where the lonely spacecraft lay immobilised, Yost was having much success in persuading the occupants to do the right thing. He had an intriguing way of semi-hypnotising them without their knowledge.

In talking to them, he had sensed that their nature was such that they were easily influenced, and after checking back through to the prime minister, he was authorised to persuade them, under full hypnosis, to return to their own planet and to destroy not only his palace but the Commander with it!

Before they were sent back on their journey, however, they were fully interrogated, and later it was clear from the readings picked up by London's sensors that a distant explosion had taken place afterwards, which could well have been the Commander's palace going up in flames and, no doubt, with him in it!

The Deputy Commander was appointed to take over straight away. He realised that there was no way that the Commander's plans could ever succeed and decided to let things cool down, as another opportunity or invention might present itself. In broadcasting to the populace, he made no wild promises but just said that he would do his best for his people. He then sent a message to Yost that his planet would no longer be a threat to any others in the galaxy, and this message was passed on with great excitement to those who'd joined in and had been supplied with what was clearly an effective deterrent—namely, the magnetite ore, the most magnetic of all the naturally occurring minerals on Earth.

Indeed, the new Commander said that he would now inform other planets in the outer galaxy that they should cooperate with any initiatives emanating from Earth, or its close satellite planets, in the future; otherwise, they would be making a great mistake.

FINAL CHAPTER

· · · · · · ● ● ● ● ● ● ● · · · · · · ·

David and Kenneth were invited to attend a major meeting to be held in the great hall adjoining the Senate in Washington DC. The UK prime minister together with other heads of government as well as delegates from all the friendly planets, whether far or near, were invited to attend, and the meeting was to be hosted by the US president himself. Most of the prime minister's PMG group also came with him, and of course, Yost and Zooba had special invitations of their own. Basil and Stephanie also received invitations for the parts they'd played in this success story, and anyone else who was still alive who had played their part were there too.

The president welcomed everyone and said, 'The world has finally reached a crossroads. The planetary system, composed of variously sized planets, each with its own traditions and cultures, has finally benefited from realising that its very existence depends on the goodwill and cooperation between each one, and I am happy to say that everyone is now acting peacefully.

'It became clear that, just as had happened on Earth, simply fighting each other failed to achieve anything in the long run. There, it became apparent that they had eventually to combine forces to see off a common enemy, namely, Mars.

'We have now reached the point where we have, as a galactic system, got to face the realistic possibility that we also face the threat of extinction, not from infighting but from natural causes destroying our planets one by one. But the fact of the matter is that we have no idea when this will take place!

'We simply have no alternative but to work together in future to ensure the survival of the planetary races, just as Earth did when it faced extinction from nuclear weapon proliferation.

'We all know that individual planets are gradually coming to the end of their natural existence, and we must ensure that before this happens, our citizens are accommodated in the surviving ones and ample arrangements are made for their peaceful integration.

'None of us knows which ones will be the first to go, so as soon as signs of impending disaster are spotted by our scientists, it is imperative that we have plans in place to accomplish a smooth transition, not necessarily from one planet to another but, quite likely, using several destinations into which populations can be absorbed each time it becomes necessary.

'There will be no infighting allowed between the original residents and the newcomers because it could well be their turn next to have to relocate themselves, and any such trouble will be taken account of when such population distributions have to take place.

'Indeed, if any fighting does occur between different groups in future, the guilty ones will be transported out to some uninhabitable place to see out their lives regretting what they have done.'

One delegate from a distant galaxy queried how this was all to be organised, and the president went on, 'We have given a great deal of thought to this, and taking the new League of Nations on Earth as an example, we propose establishing the League of Planets. It will be given wide-ranging powers and will consist of delegates from every planet who decide to join in.

'Any which refuse to do so will automatically be barred from being able to relocate to one of the others when their time comes, and this could well result in their complete extinction in the event of an overwhelming natural disaster happening there and destroying them.

'In addition to its powers of controlling such situations, the League will have its own United Planets force and a Security Council composed of delegates from the major planets, and these will be housed within a suitable establishment in Jupiter so that, between Washington and

Jupiter, there will be full control of the whole project and armed force used where necessary.'

The meeting was then thrown open to debate, but nothing material came out of it as the delegates realised that virtually everything had been thought through thoroughly in advance. They all knew where they stood and that law and order, together with justice, were now to become the norm.

Appointments of individual committees were made, each one to cover more minute details of the overall plan, and the meeting was closed after an overwhelming round of applause echoed around the room whilst those from the top table filed out.

························●··········

The president asked the prime minister to stay on to have a meal with his family, and they felt quite proud of what they had achieved. Earth's own problems had at last been resolved by cutting out bribery and corruption, and the installation of the judgebots was a success, dealing with any of those who thought they could beat the system.

He pointed out to those present that on Earth, overall control as between countries and those in them has been successful because of the new powers given to the new League of Nations, and the new relationships established with other planets such as Jupiter are a force for good. Nevertheless, the protective veil constructed around Earth had been maintained in place, just in case!

On the galactic front, there was now in place a remarkable new planetary understanding of cooperation which had never existed before.

At last, traditional attacks by Martians were a thing of the past, as were the mysterious probes from distant galaxies, searching for new accommodation for their citizens.

Members of the family gave a round of applause for all these achievements, and later on, ceremonies were held to praise the foresight of those who had, effectively, saved the world from extinction.

When the prime minister returned to London, the King asked to see him. As they sat together, the prime minister noticed the King beaming all over his face. He was absolutely delighted not only with what had been achieved but also that it had basically been done by Britain and the USA on their own, in accordance with their long-standing tradition of mutual cooperation, called their special relationship.

He went on to tell the prime minister that he was planning a ceremony at which he would be knighted for his efforts on behalf of his country and that he would shortly receive his invitation. The US president was told that he too would be invited to witness the whole ceremony.

They could expect to see a very large turnout of the populace to applaud his success, he said, and that a state visit would be arranged for him to ride down the Mall in a special coach from the royal mews, with flags flying and music playing, all the way down to Buckingham Palace for his investiture.

The prime minister hesitated for a moment whether to mention all the others who had taken part in achieving this result and what should be done about them, and the King, being acutely aware of what was going through his mind, said that he hadn't overlooked the important part they'd all played.

He was also planning, he said, to have a limited edition of a special medal struck for all those people, recording the part they had played as a memento for history. It was to have *the Justice Quotient* on its face, recording the fact that justice and law and order had finally come together, not only on Earth but also between the planets as well.

He added that the part played by alien Yost had been vital in their overall success, and something appropriate needed to be done in his case. Knighthoods and medals wouldn't be appropriate in his case, but he'd come to the conclusion that he would offer him a country estate to see out his days in comfort, if that was what he wanted. He would be allowed to bring his family, if they wanted to come, or they could use it for holiday visits only, as they wished.

They were delighted with the gift and especially that Yost's work throughout had not been overlooked, and the King was pleased that he'd found a suitable recognition for his contribution.

The prime minister came with his wife and two sons to the investiture, and at the appointed time, he knelt down to receive his medal. Before doing so, however, the King made an exceptional few public words to the gathering, pointing out how much of their success had depended on the prime minister's acumen and astuteness and that, whilst it was not right for the King to meddle in political affairs, he trusted that his party would reappoint him for another term of office, as an additional reward.

The King then leaned over, and with the special sword used for such occasions, he tapped him on the shoulder and appointed him a knight of the realm.

There was general applause from those present, and his young sons were beside themselves with delight at the thought that their Dad was now a knight!

The whole ceremony was rounded off with a grand dinner given in the Great Hall of the palace with the prime minister and his family specially placed next to the King and Queen, and warm words of approval were given in the speeches that followed.

Thus ends the saga encapsulated in the trilogy which started with *2056: Meltdown*, followed by *The Alien Veil*.

The End

THE *Shine* OF LIFE

*The Remarkable True Adventures
of a Top London Lawyer*

"...charming and unpretentious...his stories
worth sharing...are endearing and cheerful..."
– KIRKUS REVIEWS

"His style is engaging and displays a wry
humour... his accomplishments and experiences
are noteworthy and informative."
– BLUEINK REVIEWS

"...charming without sounding haughty or
arrogant... proud and eager to spread his
wisdom and philosophies..."
– U.S. REVIEW OF BOOKS

"Fans of personal memoirs or professionals
who rub shoulders with society's elite will enjoy
Altman's tale."
– FOREWORD CLARION REVIEWS

"The final verdict? Yes – a read which works on
many levels as Altman is a solid storyteller."
– PACIFIC BOOK REVIEWS

PHILIP ALTMAN

The Shine of Life

"Altman's narrative of his true-life experiences run the full gamut, from funny to bittersweet. Those expecting to pick up a dry tome of legal briefs will be very surprised by his creative content on many levels of storytelling…"
- *Pacific Book Reviews*

"Altman's memoir is breezily charming and unpretentious, and some of his stories are worth sharing…"
- *Kirkus Reviews*

"Altman's book includes not only the highlights of the author's decades as a lawyer, but his beginnings, education and personal life. His reminiscences are brief and enjoyable…"
- *BlueInk Review*

"One of Altman's most endearing qualities is that he writes about his many "adventures" without sounding arrogant or haughty; rather, he is proud and eager to spread his wisdom and his philosophies about his profession…"
- *The US Review of Books*

2056

MELTDOWN
THE LOST RULE OF LAW

PHILIP ALTMAN

2056: Meltdown

"The author has stitched together an involving mosaic of drama and suspense. Both prose and dialogue are kept crisp and concise…"
- The US Review of Books

"Rather than laying out all of the above in a scholarly diatribe or boring polemic, Altman has chosen to wrap his thesis in a rousing adventure yarn…"
- Pacific Book Review

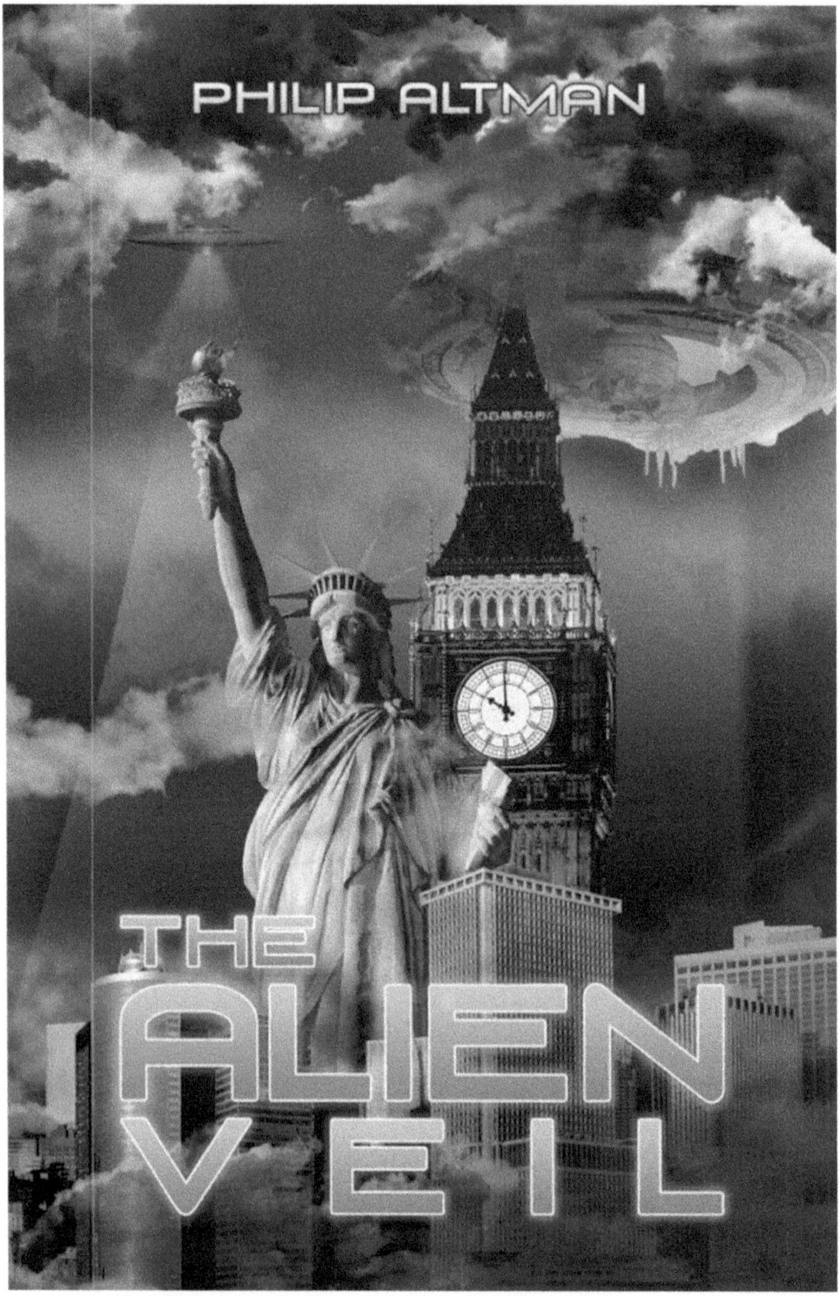
PHILIP ALTMAN
THE
ALIEN
VEIL

The Alien Veil

"The author's law career provides both a wealth of knowledge of the court system and certainly some personal insights as to its vulnerabilities and failings, making this book part spy thriller, part science fiction, and part policy suggestions..."
- The US Review of Books

Stephen Hawking once said, "To my mathematical brain, the numbers alone make thinking about aliens perfectly rational. The real challenge is to work out what aliens might actually be like." In an age where the possibility of life outside our own world seems more and more logical, author Philip Altman explores a theoretical future that sees mankind's interaction with an alien race seeking a new home at any cost in his novel, The Alien Veil. The book is a unique blend of mystery, thriller and some sci-fi elements, showcasing a world where robots are a more dominant presence in humanity's world; taking on the physical labors of the day-to-day life while humanity pursues greater objectives. Serving as a sequel to the author's previous work, 2056: Meltdown, the book explores the pursuit of justice and finding order amongst the corruption and chaos of humanity.
The author does a great job of exploring a future in which crime and law have become more defined in various nations around the world. You can see the diligent and clear cut manner in which the author speaks of the law in passages such as this, "This type of petty crime had been almost eradicated in Australia by the regular imposition of heavy sentences, and it was rare for such a case to come before the courts any more, especially in front of this appeal court." This is a novel meant for anyone who enjoys tales of alien encounters, detailed looks into legal proceedings and how future technology and knowledge can affect crime and the punishments which follow. From economic and international crimes to straight up corruption charges, Altman explores the concept of law and order thoroughly in his novel.

As someone who enjoys a good thriller and stories involving aliens from space, the novel is the perfect read. It has a healthy dose of detailed investigative writing mixed into a story of AI and robotic-based crimes, space exploration and encounters of extraterrestrial origins. There are a couple of notes I would give to the author as far as editing goes. The story itself and the characters are all fascinating to delve into.

This is a phenomenal read for any fan of the thriller or sci-fi genre. Exploring the future in a unique way, readers will love taking a peak into a possible future scenario for humanity that is both imaginable and unimaginable all at once. If you enjoy stories of fighting off corruption and the possible ramifications of meeting an alien civilization, then Philip Altman's The Alien Veil is the ideal book to transport you to a different place and time.

-Pacific Book Review

"Altman's writing is clear and concise with an unwavering momentum..."
- Kirkus Reviews

Lightning Source UK Ltd.
Milton Keynes UK
UKHW040431240219
337804UK00002B/66/P